THE
DELTA
FORCE

JOEL NORST

ST. MARTIN'S PRESS
NEW YORK

St. Martin's Press titles are available at quantity discounts for sales promotions, premiums or fund raising. Special books or book excerpts can also be created to fit specific needs. For information write to special sales manager, St. Martin's Press, 175 Fifth Avenue, New York, N.Y. 10010.

First printing/February 1986

ISBN: 0-312-90155-0
Can. ISBN: 0-312-90156-9

Cover design by George Paturzo

With special thanks to
Dennis Bacoch, Don Dorsey and
Jack Mitchell.

1

Worst scenario.

This was not happening, Scott McCoy tried to tell himself. It was only one of those *worst-scenario* nightmares he sometimes had before an operation, and he was still asleep inside his Fort Bragg quarters, his fear of failure tripping off some elaborate anxiety attack in the predawn stillness.

It was ten times brighter than day outside. He could look up into a tower of fire.

There was a peal of unnatural thunder, and for a few seconds it rained molten aluminum drops in the sand around him. One glanced off his cheek and then landed in a fold of his sleeve.

No, he realized, this was real. This was Iran, two hundred miles southeast of Tehran. And he had already failed.

Immediately before the explosion, Colonel Alexander and he had been running from helicopter to tactical transport, begging the Marine and Air Force pilots not to depart until all the Delta Force operators were loaded up with their gear. At this point Operation Eagle Claw, which had attempted to rescue the American hostages in the Iranian capital city, had been scrubbed. Quite simply, there were not enough choppers in working order to continue on toward the next phase of the mission.

Squinting against the gusts of grit raised by the engines of the waiting aircraft, McCoy watched as one of the big, ungainly Sea Stallion helicopters lifted off the desert floor. It banked lazily to the left and then appeared to slip backward, clipping one of the EC-130 Hercules tankers with its seventy-two-foot-long rotor.

There was a sound he felt in his chest more than heard. Then the helicopter turned into a fireball that began flowing around the crippled transport. Men could be seen moving through the flames, inmates of hell—beyond rescue.

Another Sea Stallion, which had just taken off, eased down again. But before its wheels had touched ground, a short man toting a medical bag had jumped out and was sprinting through the flaring light toward a Hercules crewman who was groveling in the dust to extinguish his fiery back.

McCoy and Doctor Jack, the Delta medic, began shoveling sand on the obstinate blue flickerings with their hands.

"Doc!" McCoy shouted. "Was Peterson loaded on your chopper?"

"No! There wasn't room!" He hit the crewman with a syringe. "Pete said he'd jump aboard one of the Hercs!"

McCoy saw an injured operator and ran to him. Dazed, his eyebrows scorched off, the man was clutching his HK-21 machine gun as if he suspected that the rendezvous had been ambushed. "What the fuck happened, little boss? One second I'm stowing my gear, and the next everything's on fire."

"Where's Pete?"

"I'm not sure." The operator's eyes clicked toward the white heart of the conflagration. A Redeye missle corkscrewed out of it and wobbled across the indigo sky. "I think he was up in troop seating with us."

McCoy had taken three strides toward the cargo loading ramp of the burning Hercules when Alexander cried, "McCoy! Get the hell back here!"

The major glanced over his shoulder at the ramrod-

2

straight figure—the perfect posture West Point had screamed into Nick Alexander despite his low-keyed Texas ways.

"The fuel bladders are going to blow!" Alexander tried one more time. "You know I can't wait!"

McCoy nodded that he understood, but then moved toward the ramp again. The Iranians were probably already scrambling F-4s toward Desert One.

The port wing of the Hercules was fused to the twisted wreckage of the helicopter like some wicked-looking modern sculpture. The entire side of the transport was aflame, and the metal skin had been burned away in some places, exposing a skeleton of fuselage frames.

"Peter!"

McCoy used his fatigue jacket like a cape to shield his face, but still the heat threatened to suck the air out of his lungs. His nostrils were filled with the stench of singed hair—his own. And although his jump suit was flame-resistant, he still felt like he was entering the cargo deck stark naked.

A crewman was slumped against the port paratroop door—obviously dead.

McCoy skirted a huge black rubberized bladder with a warning stenciled in yellow:

DANGER
HIGHLY FLAMMABLE.

Had everything gone right, this fuel would have been pumped into the helicopters, which would now be flying north through the night. But everything had gone wrong, and now good men were dying with no hope of success to give it meaning.

If McCoy knew Peterson, the sergeant major would have left the troop seating bay for the navigator's desk to consult the map and, hopefully, come up with some last-minute inspiration that might save Operation Eagle Claw from being aborted.

But Peterson had never made it that far.

He was sprawling across a twisted cargo floor panel, a bruise darkening half of his forehead from where the initial explosion had hurled him against a bulkhead. His leg was pinned against the bladder by the hydraulic actuator motor, which had been ripped from its moorings.

"Pete!" McCoy shouted, trying to rouse him.

The sergeant's eyelids parted a fraction of an inch, then closed again.

McCoy grasped the conduit that was still attached to the motor. Instantly, he let go and tucked his hands under his armpits. When he looked at them a moment later, his palms were puffy with blisters.

Using his fatigue jacket now, he strained to lift the pump off Peterson's leg, but the machinery proved too heavy for the purchase he could get on it with the now half-melted synthetic material. Flinging the jacket aside, tightening his jaws against the pain, he clasped the searing metal of the conduit with his bare hands and heaved the pump aside.

The agony galloped up his arms and hit his brain. "Come on, Peter!" He rolled the semiconscious man onto his back and hoisted him in a fireman's carry. "My turn now."

Last time the roles had been reversed. Peterson had carried his leg-shot lieutenant out of their overrun Green Beret camp in the highlands of Vietnam.

Staggering under the sergeant major's weight, McCoy ran for the starboard paratroop door, then leaped down into the sand, hitting hard with Peterson's bulk on top of him, nearly losing his wind.

But seeing that the last Hercules was taxiing out into the night, its ramp slowing rising like the drawbridge to a castle and knowing he had no intention of letting Peterson and himself fall into the hands of the Ayatollah, McCoy grunted to his feet and began giving chase.

Alexander was drying up the last of Desert One—he

had to get his people out of there. This misadventure on Iranian soil had been going on for hours, one delay after another, one accident heaped on top of another.

The order the boss had given was sound, McCoy reminded himself, his saliva tasting like copper as he sprinted with everything left inside him. He would have given it himself, had he been in the colonel's place.

Doctor Jack appeared at the ramp housing opening, and then Bobby Lee, a corporal, and finally Alexander himself, who joined the others in shouts of encouragement that McCoy could not hear over the roar of the turbo-props.

The ramp was nearly perpendicular when he was still thirty feet behind it. With Peterson beginning to slide down off his back, McCoy made it to within an arm's reach of the rising platform. He twisted his trunk sideways so Doctor Jack and Bobby could seize Peterson by his jump suit and haul him aboard.

All at once McCoy was 170 pounds lighter. But the sudden shift in his center of gravity cost him his balance.

In the instant that he spread-eagled on the thin layer of sand that was shifting across the underlying hardpan, McCoy thought: *My God, I'm going to have to hoof it five hundred miles to the Turkish border!*

The lip of the ramp had elevated another foot by the time he could catch up with the Hercules again.

Lunging up as high as his legs would spring him, he caught the edge under his arms.

Either Alexander's frantic yank on McCoy's body harness or his own straddling kick carried the major over the top. He skidded down into the red-lit dimness of the aircraft's interior as the ramp clanged shut.

Even over the revving of the Hercules's engines, he heard when the fuel bladders finally blew on the stricken EC-130.

Then, after a jarring bump, they were wheels up and climbing steeply.

Doctor Jack went back to tending a badly burned Marine pilot. Peterson, he thought, would be all right.

Colonel Alexander was staring through the closed ramp as if it were made of glass. His eyes were still filled with the flaming wreckage of Desert One.

McCoy took stock of the wounded, murmured a few soft words, patted a few shoulders, then sagged into a troop seat. His hands were throbbing. But Doctor Jack was working furiously to stabilize the pilot, so the major said nothing.

The pilot quickly leveled off. As in its approach to the desert rendezvous, the squadron would fly at four hundred feet, hopefully below Iranian radar.

Operation Eagle Claw was concluded—even before it had begun.

Alexander lowered himself into the seat beside McCoy. Their eyes did not meet. Ten minutes later the colonel said just loud enough to be heard over the engine noise, "What the hell are the American people going to think? My God, Scott, how can we explain what happened here tonight?"

McCoy was silent for a long moment. "When I was a kid—"

"Michigan," Alexander interrupted, as if McCoy had just rescued him from some pretty grim thoughts. "Aren't you from Michigan?"

"Upper Peninsula." He pressed his hands under his arms again. "I must've been eleven or twelve. My old man let me take out his sailboat for the first time alone. Well, I did everything perfect. But on the way back into the harbor, a motor job—a big one from Chicago—cut me off. I had the right of way. But the rich sons of bitches forced me up onto the jetty rocks . . ." McCoy fell silent. "My old man said it didn't matter if I was in the right or dead wrong. My hand was on the tiller when she went aground."

Alexander closed his eyes.

McCoy got up and went aft. Something had snapped inside, something he felt sure that could never be patched up again. From now on he was just going to bide his time. He'd joined the Army at seventeen. In five years he'd have twenty years in. Until that day, when he might raise horses and forget how the politicians could hamstring one of the best military units in the world, he was just going to bide his time.

Bobby Lee was squatting under the troop water bottles, weeping bitterly. McCoy envied the young operator. He himself was too heartsick to cry.

2

14 June 1985 . . . 0830 Hours . . . Cairo

Tom Hale realized that, even had the gunnery sergeant not tagged along in his blues, the largely Arab crowd milling around outside the international flights terminal still would have known that he and his two buddies, Ed Jones and Andy Thatcher, were American Marines. One look at the whitewall haircuts was enough to make beggar waifs cry, "John Wayne! Give me dollah, buckaroo!" Ed, whose features were somewhat delicate, almost Ethiopian, elicited a shout of "Michael Jackson!" —to the delight of Andy, who used to hide Ed's left-hand dress glove until Jones was nearly late to a watch because of the prank.

Now, as they strode toward the luggage counter, an Egyptian Air Force officer came strutting from the opposite direction. The three lance corporals followed the gunny's cue and saluted—although they wore sports jackets, ties and dark slacks, standard wear for Marine security guards when off duty.

Almost crossly, the Egyptian returned their courtesy.

Once past him the Marines traded smirks. As one of America's "ambassadors in blue," an MSG turned a lot of cheek. He walked the extra mile. To do otherwise was to risk an international incident.

But now their thirty-two-month tour was over, and the gunny had come along to say good-bye "to three of the best watch standers I've ever had," as he had told the ambassador when the trio shook his hand for the last time.

Ed Jones had re-upped. After thirty days leave, he was headed for an aviation school in Memphis—"and that's Memphis, *Tennessee,* not fucking Egypt," he told Tom at the farewell bash safely concealed from Moslem eyes inside the Marine House. "If I got to stand in a little cubicle for eight hours, I want some scenery moving past my toes and a rotor wop-wop-wopping over my head." He was referring to the agony of standing watch in Post One —the bullet-resistant glass enclosure at the main entrance to the embassy.

Andy was simply getting out. His only ambition was to wash down a ton of Puget Sound oysters with an equal weight of Rainier beer back home in Seattle.

Tom had raised a lot of eyebrows when, at last night's party he finally confessed that he'd been admitted to the freshman class at Yale. "Well, kiss my yuppie!" Ed had yowled. But in his own way, with a slight smile, he let Tom know he was pleased that his buddy since their Camp Pendleton miseries had done well for himself.

"*Semper fi,*" Ed had said, clicking his beer mug against Tom's.

But no one was more surprised about this turn of events than Tom Hale himself, especially after amassing a half dozen incompletes in a junior college career that had lasted only two months. The Corps and—yes, he had to admit to himself—Egypt had changed things for him. He'd arrived in Cairo in the middle of a Chinese fire drill with over five thousand university students pressing against the front gates, screaming, "Death to America and to Israel!" The breeze off the Nile was sharp with tear gas, and an Egyptian military helicopter kept strafing the crowd with a garbled public-address warning even the Egyptians couldn't understand. For a few minutes Tom had been unsure that it was Tehran all over again—and he wondered how his folks would take the news of his captivity, the crush of reporters that would suddenly lay siege to their adobe bungalow in Tucson.

But then the Cairo riot police came to the rescue with a water cannon that bowled over more students than a surprise physics exam.

For weeks after this incident, Tom felt confused and somewhat angry. Why did these people his own age so hate his country? He worked up the nerve to ask one of the Egyptian secretaries, and in answer to his question she started choosing books for him from the embassy library: the Koran, histories of the ebb and flow of Islam, accounts of European colonialism in the region. And in trying to understand others, he got a grip on his own emotions. He not only kept a cool head throughout a tough year for American interests in the Middle East, he also became fascinated by Arab history, enough to want to study it full-time.

The gunny now halted them near the departure counter. "All right, I guess this is it." He made his voice a little gruffer because his eyes had moistened. "And none too soon—I'm tired of mothering you bastards." He shook each of their hands with feeling. "Good luck."

And the sergeant turned on his heels and quick-marched away.

"That, my friends," Ed said softly, "is pure pride riding on a pair of spit-shined shoes."

"Amen." Tom then realized that a boy of perhaps ten years, unmistakably American, was staring at him. "Hi. What's up?"

"Nothing. Are you soldiers too?"

"Marines—yes. My name's Tom. What's yours?"

"Jay."

The boy's mother intervened. "I'm sorry. He just talks to everybody."

"He's not bothering me." Tom tousled the boy's hair. At that moment boarding was announced for his row. The staff made sure embassy personnel got preassigned seating —another precaution against Americans being too visible. "See you around, Jay."

"Sure."

Passing through glass doors, finding himself suddenly outside the sway of air conditioning, Tom squinted against the brash sunlight and almost reflexively shooed a fly away from his eyes.

The waiting aircraft was a Boeing 727—not exactly as comfortable as a 747, but it would do? It was *home-bound* after stopovers in Athens and Rome.

Leading the way, Tom bounded up the ramp into the plane, where the line slowed while the stewardesses directed each passenger to his seat. Briefly, he had a glimpse of the instrument-cluttered cabin. The pilot and co-pilot had reassuring wisps of gray in their hair. The flight engineer was blocked from view by the open door.

"Welcome to ATW," one of the stewardesses said to Tom. Great smile. She was pretty, enough so to make him wonder if he had blushed, even slightly, when he first looked at him. "I am Gretti Werner, your purser on today's flight. Please don't hesitate to call your stewardess or me if you need anything."

"Thank you," Tom said. She had a soft German accent, but Tom knew how to make sure diplomatically. "Swiss?"

That fetching smile burst across her face. "No . . . Munich." She glanced at his ticket. "Your seat is all the way to the back."

As the Marines passed fleetingly through the first-class cabin, Ed Jones sighed wistfully, "I bet this is where the dogfaces get to sit—hors d'oeuvres . . . champagne."

But Tom saw no American soldiers settled back in the wide seats. Instead, a young Egyptian with the pensive look of a student but the tweedy threads of a junior professor glanced up from a book—and hardened his gaze on Tom, who let his own eyes blear to indifference.

A resurgence of Islamic fervor is nothing new under the Middle Eastern sun, he reminded himself. *Don't take it personally.*

In the tourist-class cabin, the Marines sidestepped into their row. The three seats across the aisle from them were being occupied by young Jay and his slow-moving parents, who now looked like they'd spent their vacation chasing the ten-year-old up and down the Giza Pyramids.

Andy, still recovering from last night, immediately buckled up and shut his eyes. Ed scanned the card of emergency instructions, but then frowned and replaced it in the pouch. "I'll wait for the movie."

Tom found himself eavesdropping on the people seated directly forward of him: a Roman Catholic priest, a nun and a foreigner who, at a passing glance, had seemed a very bad dresser.

"It is a nice coincidence we are both from Chicago," this man now said to the priest.

Tom ran the accent through the mental catalogue of those he had heard as an MSG. It was definitely COM-BLOC—but *which* communist country escaped him.

"Do you know of the St. Catherine's Church by Lincoln Park?"

"Yes, Father Duchinsky's," the priest said pleasantly.

"I go there every Sunday since I left Russia four years ago."

The man said this shrilly enough for Tom to suspect that he was trying to cover up a growing case of nerves.

"Well, I must tell Ivan when I see him at our next

11

Council of Churches meeting. I'm Father O'Malley, and this is Sister Mary."

"Very much a pleasure . . . David Hoffman."

Tom nodded to himself. No non-Arab felt completely at ease traveling in the Middle East. The feeling was probably doubled for Jews.

Tom's eyes darted up to the speaker above his head. "This is Captain Roger Campbell. I'd like to welcome everyone aboard ATW flight 827 from Cairo to New York via Athens and Rome. We've just been cleared for takeoff. Our flying time will be ninety minutes to Athens, where it's sunny with eighty-seven degrees. I'll remind you that the no-smoking signs are lit . . ."

Tom leaned the side of his head against the window. A few minutes later, the ascent pressing on him, he watched a tilting expanse of cultivated land pass below— the delta of the Nile. With its date palms, citrus groves and alfalfa fields, the country reminded him of southern Arizona—except that along that yellow-brown ribbon of river now shimmering under the morning sun, exactly one hundred years before British General Charles Gordon had lost his life and his command to a flash flood of Islamic fury.

There is nothing new under the Middle Eastern sun. He closed his eyes and tried to catch a few winks.

0030 Hours . . . North Carolina

Creedence Clearwater was blasting from the house. Scott McCoy could ignore it, until the sounds of breaking glass made him glare through the yawning barn doors at the brightly lit windows of his own place. Hopefully, just another empty bottle of Jack Daniel's being chucked into the fireplace.

So far everything was under relative control, although during the chorus of "Looking Out My Back Door," Bobby Lee had thrust his head right through the screen door and bawled, "Hey, little boss! This is Staff Sergeant Robert Lee! Get your ass back in here before I get nasty!" Then he lost his balance and fell forward, ripping the frame off its hinges. Staggering to his feet, he giggled and—for reasons that were entirely his own—ran around the side of the farmhouse, wearing the door like a dickey.

Even a year ago, McCoy would have been inside, keeping up with the worst of the revelers, enjoying every minute of Delta Force shoptalk. But in a very real sense he no longer belonged. As of two weeks ago, Major Scott McCoy could put the abbreviation for retired in brackets behind his name. And whatever that meant, he would find out in due time.

Well, he decided, taking a pause from stroking his horse's nose, *perhaps it means all this: forty acres of pine and pasture butting up on Uwharrie National Forest, a sabot in a corner of the barn I can sail on Badin Lake after I reglass the hull, and no more Washington politicians cutting the legs out from under me.*

So it was time to pull back from Delta Force. Sever all the emotional ties—cleanly.

Despite the massive decibel level of the stereo he'd bought in Saigon nearly two decades before, McCoy heard the rustling of clothing just before Pete Peterson said, "Three months of living out here alone and you'll go buggy."

"Try me."

Nancy, Peterson's fiancée, a bank teller in Fayetteville, was tucked under the sergeant major's arm. Her face, a little flushed from drinking, took on an apologetic look. "I'm sorry about the mess they're making inside, Scott."

McCoy tried to smile. "Didn't this lug tell you? Tonight is an ice cream social compared to most of our wingdings." Through the corner of his eye, he saw Peterson urge her with a nod to go back inside. She pouted, but he smoothed it over with a kiss.

McCoy stepped inside the stall, grabbed a brush, and began going through the horse's mane for tangles.

Peterson made sure Nancy was inside before asking, "You hiding out here because you're afraid you're going to miss us too bad?"

McCoy said nothing.

"Now, lookee here, Major—"

"*Retired,*" he snapped.

"Oh, bullshit, you won't last sixty days out here sanding that dingy of yours and raking up pasture pastries. Nothing's perfect. And God knows, Scottie, our business ain't—"

"But it has to *mean* something." McCoy said this so fiercely that Peterson closed his mouth and looked down. "We beat back the Tet offensive, gave the bastards enough casualties to cripple their war machine for years—but some idiots in Washington put their heads together and decided we'd lost and it was time to negotiate. And five years ago we left eight good men behind in the Iranian desert because the same idiots wanted to prance between the raindrops instead of going balls-out. America doesn't need a counterterrorist group, right? We got a huge nuclear arsenal, right? Shit, did that arsenal save us from having to gouge out our eyes with our fingers in Nam? Shit, as usual we're preparing for the kind of war we'll probably never have to fight. Terrorism's the most common form of modern battle. But who can you tell that to in Washington? Peter"—McCoy pointed the brush at him —"when you're never allowed to succeed, the struggle loses its meaning. And you wind up just going through the motions. I can't live that way anymore."

14

Peterson began to say something, but then he thought better of it and slowly ambled back toward the house. Halfway there, he halted and said over his shoulder, "I wish you wouldn't call me Peter. Only you and my god-damned mother call me Peter."

McCoy smiled despite himself.

4

1010 Hours . . . Athens

Toolbox in hand, the maintenance man jumped down from the electric cart. He thanked the driver with a wave, then hurried up the ramp into the port rear service door of Flight 827.

The only sound within was the faint humming of the air-conditioning fans. The few passengers who had elected to remain aboard during the layover were dozing or reading.

At the far end of the aisle, the cockpit door was shut. None of the crew could be seen in the tourist-class cabin.

"Excuse me . . ." an elderly American woman delayed him by the sleeve, "do you speak English?"

"Yes, madam." His heart began trip-hammering. He eyed the nearby doors of the aft lavatories. The overhead sign indicated that at least one of them was unoccupied— but that might not be for long.

"Please tell me something." Refusing to let go of him, she leaned toward the window, which was two vacant seats away. "Can the Parthenon be seen from here?"

"No, madam, the Acropolis cannot be seen from here."

"Even on a clear day?"

"I am sorry . . ." He walked out of her grasp, checked the aisle for the crew one more time, then slipped inside the port restroom—the starboard one was taken. He fumbled to secure the latch behind him. Setting his toolbox on the commode, he paused a moment to take several deep breaths. Fanning out his fingers, he waited until their trembling was under control before taking a sharp-bladed screwdriver from the box and gently prying loose the faceplate on the paper towel dispenser. Pulling out sheath after sheath of paper, he reached the spring-loaded plate under the bottom most towel, jiggled it free and laid it athwart the small basin.

This left an empty space, and he swiftly moved to fill it. Two Russian-made fragmention hand grenades and a nickel-plated 9mm Beretta pistol went into the bottom. The silver plating would make the handgun eye-catching —a definite asset. Next, he laid in two magazines of twenty .32 ACP rounds each. Finally he carefully inserted a Czechoslovakian-made Scorpion submachine gun in the cavity, resting the barrel at an angle so there would still be room for a layer of towels. An American-made MAC-10 would have been easier to conceal, but none was available on the market.

At first his clients had given him a Hungarian AMD, really just a shortened version of the Kalashnikov rifle. When he protested that it was impossible to hide such a weapon in the limited space given, they'd offered him more money—as if more money would make the towel dispenser bigger. For this and a hundred other reasons, he preferred doing business with Palestinians. They usually had an appreciation for what was possible. But at the present time the Shia Lebanese had lots of money in their pockets. Iranian probably—but was that any reason not to divert a little before it dried up?

Leaving enough towels to accommodate at least half an hour's worth of visits by passengers, he tapped the faceplate back into place, made sure he was leaving nothing suspicious behind and stepped out into the aisle at the same moment the opposite lavatory door also swung open.

A stewardess looked at him quizzically. "What is it?" she asked in passable Greek, but with a German accent.

"Report of a leak from the faucet. But I can find nothing wrong. How is the one in that lavatory?"

Finally she broke off her stare. "Fine, I think."

"Well, then, perhaps they should be checked again in Rome." Slowly, although everything inside him begged his feet to hurry, he shuffled a few feet, then stalled. He could feel the stewardess's eyes on him.

He smiled at the American woman who had spoken to him before. "Is this your first time to Athens?"

"Yes—but I'm afraid your smog looks like what we have in Los Angeles."

"A pity for both our cities." He pressed his lips together. The portside lavatory door had clicked shut. The German bitch had gone inside to check! But he continued to smile at the American woman. "This pollution is eating away our beautiful monuments." He knew it would do no good to run. Better to bluff his way through—even if caught seemingly red-handed. He had shared some of the Shi'ite windfall with a few higher-ups for such an eventuality.

At last the stewardess came out. She glared at him, but he knew she had found nothing.

"Well, madam," he said to the elderly woman as he moved toward the ramp again, "you must come back to Greece someday."

Abdul had been advised by an experienced brother not to lapse into a distracted appearance while waiting overnight at the terminal. At five that morning he had used the public restroom to trim his curly black beard and comb his equally unruly hair. He was a Levantine merchant, after all, and such a Sunni dog gave greater attention to his appearance than his virtue. Restored to his respectable incognito, he took his place on the bench nearest the newsstand in the departure lounge, having shunned any of the Arab-language dailies in favor of the *London Times*.

Unconsciously, his hand checked for his pistol in the waistband of his shiny slacks. He recoiled before he recalled that the piece was packed away inside his quarters at the Bekaa Valley barracks—along with a packet of clean white cloth containing verses he had selected from the Koran that, he felt, best described the spirit of the martyrdom he was willing to accept this morning.

Mustafa was sprawled across a bench three rows away, feigning sleep. Or perhaps he genuinely was asleep. Affectionately, Abdul chuckled to himself. Mustafa was truly a Shia boy—a hewer of wood and a drawer of water, as rich Beirut Moslems liked to call the Shi'ites from Jabal Amil, the traditional Shia homeland in southern Lebanon so recently ravaged by the Israelis. Abdul despised these prosperous Sunni Lebanese almost as much as he hated Maronite Christians and their Zionist puppeteers.

Abdul could see that Mustafa's chest was no longer rising and falling. The youth was holding his breath. The obese plainclothes security agent was making his predictable rounds again through the waiting areas. Abdul checked his Bulova: another thirty minutes to departure.

The security agent waddled on toward the next stop on his clockwork schedule.

Mustafa was a member of the Shia militia, Amal, as Abdul had once been. But after one terrible day two years before, Amal had proved too moderate to suit his rage. Allah—the compassionate, the merciful—had stricken the visages of Abdul's wife and daughter from his mind so as not to endlessly torture him with the sweet memory of them. Instead, when their dead names crossed his tongue, Abdul saw only the fortresslike profile of the *New Jersey*, the flashes from its great guns, and then the explosions in the wooded hills above Beirut—smoke gushing up out of the Druze village where Abdul had believed his family would be safe.

Abdul had left Amal and joined the most dedicated faction of Hizbollah, the Party of God, entrenched under Syrian protection in the Bekaa Valley.

But today's bloodshed would be waged under the banner of Islamic Jihad, the Moslem Holy War—not so much an organization as a cover name for combined operations against the Israelis and their American backers. Jihad had taken credit for the bombings of the American Embassy and Marine headquarters, although martyrs from Abdul's own unit of Hizbollah had executed the attacks.

It was announced in Greek and then English: "El Al Flight 257 from Tel Aviv has landed. Passengers will be disembarking from Gate 35."

The waiting had become insufferable. Abdul decided to stroll over and watch these Zionists return from wailing at their ruin of a wall.

The first El Al passengers to come puffing through the doors were obviously a family: a man and woman in their midsixties; by a strong resemblance to his father, their son and his wife; and finally a small dark-haired girl of perhaps six years. Abdul's heart ached for an instant.

"Kaplan . . . the name is Benjamin Kaplan," the old man said to the clerk at the El Al departure desk, as if that should mean something special. "Please make sure of our luggage—I beg you. We've got a tight connection. Where does the ATW flight to New York depart?"

"Gate 37, sir—"

"There it is, Dad," the young man said, briefly eyeing Abdul before picking up his daughter and herding his parents and wife toward the Flight 827 waiting area.

Abdul decided it was not so easy to tell American Jews. Most often they looked bored and fat like other Americans. And to make matters more difficult, they had Slavic names. German names. Even English names.

The public address came to life again: "ATW Flight 827 is now ready for boarding at Gate 37. Rows 15 through 30 will board at this time."

That was Jaffar's signal. The third member of the squad would now move to board the aircraft. Abdul stepped around a pillar so he could peer down the long corridor toward the metal-detector station.

"Where are you?" he growled softly as the seconds ticked away and the lean half-Druze, half-Palestinian youth failed to show.

Jaffar Ibn Khalil, he felt, was their weakest link. Son of a Palestinian father and a Druze mother—in itself an oddity because of the Druze misgivings against intermarriage—he had fallen under the sway of the PLO, even fought beside Arafat's Al-Fatah during the Israeli invasion of Lebanon. But when the PLO was forced to leave Beirut, Jaffar stayed behind and shifted his immature loyalties to a Druze militia unit.

His chief fame in revolutionary circles came from having blown up a Middle East Airlines Boeing 707 with a Soviet-made RPG-7V rocket. For this questionable achievement, he had been included in today's mission, although Abdul had reminded the coalition leadership that no rockets would be used—and Jaffar had a well-deserved reputation for being hot-headed.

At last the young man could be seen standing in line to pass through the metal detector.

Jaffar had picked up his ticket at the last minute.

Abdul could sense the presence of Mossad everywhere. And if not the Israeli intelligence service, the CIA. And if not the Americans, Interpol. The three men had purchased their tickets separately and at different times. They had also decided not to wait in the terminal like a pack of wolves, licking their teeth to pounce on Flight 827.

Jaffar's turn came to pass through the detector. He breezed through and was five paces closer to the departure lounge when the uniformed woman called for him to halt.

20

Fool! Abdul thought to himself. *He has tried to carry a pistol through!*

The woman held out a small tray to Jaffar, and he deposited a fistful of what appeared to be coins or foiled-wrapped chocolate candies on it. His second trip through the sensor, made with a defiant grin, set off no alarms. He retrieved his property and continued on his way.

Exhaling at last, Abdul turned. Jaffar was not the only man he had been waiting to see. And there, tinkering with the drinking fountain outside the men's restroom, was the contemptible Greek in his maintenance jump suit. When the Reign of Virtue was ushered in, mercenary vermin of this ilk would be eliminated. But now Abdul was relieved to watch the Greek clasp his hand to the back of his neck as if massaging away a crick. The awaited signal: all was ready aboard the plane.

A voice was being raised in anger at the ATW counter. Abdul pretended to take no interest in the argument that, all at once, was raging there—for the loud voice belonged to Jaffar.

"But I have been buying this ticket at the front not moments ago!"

"I'm sorry, sir," the young woman from ATW said. "This flight is full."

"But your company giving me this ticket!" He waved it in her face, his olive-colored cheeks now underlaid with crimson.

"I'm sorry, but yours is a standby ticket."

"This was not told to me!"

Then a male clerk said to Jaffar, "We *are* full, sir. Please stand aside."

Abdul saw that Mustafa had risen from his bench and was gaping at the confrontation. Before he could motion for Mustafa to take no extraordinary interest in it, Jaffar began charging for the loading gate.

"Phone!" the male agent told the young woman as he lunged for Jaffar, catching him by the coat sleeve.

"Away!" Jaffar snarled, seizing the agent by the shoulders and bowling him over. But the man refused to let go of Jaffar, and they both rolled onto the floor.

Within seconds security policemen arrived. Forcibly, they disentangled a screaming and kicking Jaffar from the clerk, who now had a bloodied mouth.

"What are we to do?" Mustafa whispered from behind Abdul.

"Nothing. We board."

5

1050 Hours . . . Over the Gulf of Corinth

Abdul slumped on the commode, knee deep in crumpled wads of paper towels. He bit the webbing between his thumb and forefinger, hard, before jamming his forearm down into the empty cavity of the dispenser once again.

His eyes widened as he experienced a slight floating sensation. The plane was leveling off at its cruising altitude.

Betrayed—there seemed room in his head for no other thoughts. But all at once he imagined what might have happened and bolted out into the aisle.

The OCCUPIED sign was lit on the opposite lavatory door. Nevertheless, he jiggled it. The latch was securely locked.

Mustafa was staring back at him from his seat in the cabin, and Abdul wondered if his own face looked as pallid and clammy as his comrade's.

In truth, Jaffar's capture had thoroughly shaken him. He felt no less fearless, no less willing to die for Shia brotherhood, but for the first time a premonition of failure trickled down his spine like ice water.

The OCCUPIED light winked out, and a young man exited the lavatory, frowning at Abdul for having tested the latch. *American,* Abdul quickly decided, *perhaps military—one to be watched.*

The man started to say something, but Abdul brushed past him and slammed the door.

He hesitated, sucked in a sharp breath that seethed between his clenched teeth, repeating over and over again in his heart of hearts: *A man can soar on the wings of sacrifice or he can submit and sink into betrayal.*

Then he grasped the exposed towels and yanked. All of them came away, no more than a two-inch stack of them, revealing the underlying plate, which he hurriedly removed. His hand wriggled down into the darkness.

He shut his eyes, laughing softly as his fingers felt the trigger housing of the Scorpion. Out came the submachine gun, then the two magazines, one of which he tucked in his waistband; the other he slapped into the weapon. The grenades and Beretta he dumped in a coat pocket. The weight of it made that side of the garment hang almost to his knee.

But appearances no longer mattered.

He and Mustafa were on the verge of soaring.

Scarcely bothering to conceal the Scorpion SMG under his coat, he abandoned the lavatory and rushed up the aisle, ignoring the attention his haste and grim expression were drawing.

Mustafa was on his feet, clawed hands outstretched to receive the SMG, the spare magazine and a grenade.

A woman shrieked.

Excellent, Abdul thought as he drew the silver-colored Beretta out of his pocket. *No sound demoralizes a man as quickly as a woman's scream.*

As they had practiced, Mustafa and he now smartly charged their weapons.

"What's going on?" a male voice demanded authoritatively.

In answer Abdul spun around, brandishing a grenade in one hand and the pistol in the other, waving them above his head so all could see. "This is a hijacking!" he cried in English so loudly his voice immediately turned raspy. "Down! Stay down or you die!"

"Put your hands on your heads!" Mustafa screamed from behind. He was swinging the Scorpion from side to side so all could have an opportunity to gaze down the black hole of its muzzle. "Put your heads on your knees!"

Another woman screamed. The shock of what was happening rippled forward through the tourist-class cabin, keeping pace with Abdul and Mustafa as they worked their way toward the cockpit.

"What's the meaning—?"

"No one talks!" Abdul realized too late that he was charging the pistol once again. An unspent cartridge was spit out onto the carpet, making his anger more vehement. "No one moves! We will blow up the plane if you resist us! You must do as we say! This is a hand grenade!"

"Doing always as we say!" Mustafa echoed. "We have grenades!"

Glancing forward, Abdul saw that a stewardess was blocking the aisle, her arms braced between the backs of two seats. "Are you crazy?" she asked. "What are you doing?"

Grasping her face with his fingers, he hurled her across the laps of three passengers. Her head struck the cabin wall, and she began moaning. When he wiped the sweat off his brow, his hand smelled of her face powder.

"Stay down!" he cried at the astonished passengers. "Down! Down—or you die!" And they bowed over the dazed stewardess.

The woman who had introduced herself at the beginning of the flight as the purser now wheeled a tray from the galley out into the first-class cabin. Abdul surprised her from behind, grasping a handful of her brown hair. Dismayed, on the brink of anger, she tried to turn—but was halted by the muzzle of the Beretta, which was denting her cheek. "This is a hijacking! We go now to the cockpit!"

A passenger bolted up out of his seat. Only after he had pounded him across the temple with the butt of the pistol did Abdul recognize his victim as the young man who had arrived in Athens on the El Al flight. He collapsed across his wife's knees.

"I kill him!" Abdul touched his pistol to the back of the insensible man's head. "I kill him now!"

"Oh, God, please!" the woman begged, her husband's blood fanning out across her pink skirt. Her daughter had covered her ears with her hands, her little mouth widened by a piercing scream.

"Stop it! Everyone stop!" Abdul swung the Beretta back into the purser's face, then pushed her ahead of him with his fist, which still grasped a grenade.

They halted before the cockpit door. "Tell them to open it up," Abdul said in a low voice for the first time. "Open it up or we explode the plane. My friend and I are prepared to die."

Her face lost its color, but she said, "The captain will never open the door if he thinks there's trouble."

She had looked down at her intertwined fingers; Abdul now lifted her chin with the muzzle. "Then you must assure the captain all is well."

She picked up the intercom phone, licked her lips as she waited—then again. "Jim, it's me . . . no, everything's okay." Then, resting her forehead against the wall, she closed her eyes and hung up.

There followed a faint rattle from the latch. The door cracked open no more than an inch when Abdul, followed closely by Mustafa, burst into the cockpit, throwing the flight engineer against his console. In the same instant Mustafa spun aftward, covering the aisle with the Scorpion, Abdul yanked the pin out of a grenade and shoved the drab-green cylinder under the pilot's nose.

"I get your point," the man said.

His coolness made Abdul smile. "Excellent. I am taking over command of this aircraft."

"And you are—?"

"Colonel Abdul of the Musa al Sadr Brigade of Islamic Jihad." Suddenly Abdul swung his pistol on the co-pilot. He had seen the man activate some kind of switch under the lip of the instrument panel. "What is that? What are you doing?"

"Autopilot," the captain answered. "Whenever there's an emergency of this kind, we go on autopilot until it's resolved."

Abdul's eyes narrowed. "Well, take it off—at once! All—as of this minute—is quite resolved!"

The co-pilot's right hand darted for the switch again.

"You are to fly to Beirut. As long as you follow my orders, there will be no emergency."

Abdul looked out through the windscreen and then up through the eyebrow windows. He suppressed a grin. Nothing but open, sunlit sky to soar across. *"Allah Akbar,"* he whispered fervently. *God is Great.*

0215 Hours . . . North Carolina

Nick Alexander liked to jog at night, especially when it would help burn off four shots of Bushmills Irish, drunk neat—except for two Heineken backs. Now, running down an asphalt path buckled by the roots of huge elms, unconsciously counting the cones of the bug-streaked streetlights he passed through every hundred meters, he began to feel pretty good. The scenery seemed to slip past faster than it did in the daylight. He was already approaching the park surrounding the pond. The darkness over the water was being pricked by fireflies. It seemed a little early in the season for fireflies.

He'd already packed away his sweat pants. The humidity, now so velvety and cool against his face, would turn surly on him—the good old Fort Bragg summer.

Then, as if it belonged to a quick-draw artist instead of a forty-eight-year-old Army officer, his hand flashed to his side even before the third beep had escaped the clip-on device. The closest secure phone, he decided, was at the Stockade, Delta Force's headquarters. He stretched it out, picked up the pace to seven-minute miles. But with no vehicles on the road at this hour to flag down, it took him ten minutes to reach the guard at the main entrance.

He was three steps inside the door when Staff Sergeant Winnemucca, one of the on-duty operators, gave him the night's classified number by which he could reach the Joint Task Force commander at the Pentagon. "Thanks, Waukene. Where's the duty officer?"

"He's already on the horn to Pope, sir."

"Good," Alexander murmured. Delta always had one of its three HC-130 tactical transports on standby at nearby Pope Air Force Base; the lieutenant was phoning to roust the crew. Keeping the twelve digits in his head, Alexander locked the door in his office, then sat down to dial. His heart was still pounding—the running, he told himself.

It was answered on the first ring. "Crisis Management Command Center, Lieutenant Colonel Gomez speaking, sir."

"Alexander here."

"One moment, Colonel."

Carl Woodbridge's voice boomed through the receiver. "Nick?"

"Hello, General." They'd been classmates at West Point, Woodbridge graduating seventeen rungs beneath Alexander in the long, gray pecking order. But Woodbridge had gone the Pentagon corridor route instead of jumping out of the ass ends of airplanes—and that was why he had two stars glittering on his collar and Alexander had none. "What've you got for us?"

"Could be a righteous one, Nick."

Alexander almost repeated the word in an ironic tone of voice. He blamed the urge on the Bushmills—God's magic potion for keeping the Irish from taking over the world.

"Athens Airport picked up an emergency hijacking alert signal about fifteen minutes ago," Woodbridge went on. "I was already down here. We were on a practice alert—"

"What carrier, sir?"

"ATW—Athens to New York with a Rome stopover. About a hundred Americans aboard."

Alexander did a quick mental calculation. It was about ten in the morning over the Adriatic. "Destination still Rome?"

"Negative. We're tracking the flight eastward. Beirut or Damascus, maybe. Someone's even suggested our terrorists, who remain unidentified, want to make a suicide crash landing in Tel Aviv."

Alexander reached down and took the sweaty pack of Winstons out of his athletic sock—he always finished a run with a cigarette, if only to prove to himself that he was still a paratrooper at heart, not some health faddist. As he lit up, he was already processing Woodbridge's information.

These were the moments in which he first stumbled inside the Maze, that labyrinth of rumors, guestimates and fabrications he had to try to outsmart at ground level.

Later, after the dust had settled and the entire picture was crystal clear to even the biggest dummy in Washington, he would be asked why he hadn't done this and hadn't done that—as if, during these bewildering first steps, he had had an aerial view, a map of every twist and turn in the Maze.

". . . so, Nick," Woodbridge concluded, "put Delta Force on Phase Three Alert. Fly to the Middle East."

"Sicily? Egypt? Israel?"

"We'll advise. And Nick—the President just told me he doesn't want another Tehran."

Alexander snuffed out his smoke. He almost said: *Then tell the President to have his old lady pack him a lunch. He can come along.* The Bushmills again. "He won't have one, sir, if Delta can help it."

"Good luck, pal," Woodbridge said with a warm tone of voice Alexander hadn't heard in thirty years.

"Thanks, Carl."

He had a million things to do and an impossibly brief time in which to do them. But first he phoned information and asked for what was probably a new rural listing.

Momentarily disentangling himself from Nancy's embrace, ignoring her little whine, Peterson looked up over the top of the front seat of the old Eldorado convertible. Bobby Lee was sitting very straight. Too straight. And his eyes were as wide as they could open. "Bobby, how you doing?"

"Fine." And he sounded fine too. The forcible dunking in the stock trough at McCoy's farm must have helped.

But then Peterson looked through the windshield. He bolted upright, the breeze hitting him full in the face. "If you're doing so goddamn fine, why are we in the goddamn oncoming lane!"

"Because we're on the four-lane between Pinehurst and Southern Pines." Bobby sounded a bit offended, but he continued to gaze forward, hands primly at ten and two o'clock on the wheel.

"Sorry, buddy." Peterson eased back down and joined his mouth to Nancy's. He was on the verge of kissing her closed eyelids when it hit him—they'd sped through Southern Pines thirty minutes before.

But before he could do anything, the convertible's windshield lit up like white phosphorous and a horn was wailing in inexorable approach. An instant later the Eldorado was bouncing off the road, and he was holding on to Nancy with genuine desperation for the first time that evening. "Jesus!"

Somehow, miraculously, Bobby Lee had skidded the car to a sideways halt without overturning it. The engine had stalled out.

Peterson and Nancy sat in each other's clutches as a pall of dust descended over them.

"My mistake," Bobby said quietly. Then, after a soft hiccup: "You want to drive?"

"Jesus Christ!" Peterson cried, lunging over the seat and seizing Nancy's purse with both hands. He dumped the contents into his lap. "Jesus H. Christ!" At last he found the beeper and turned it off. "How long—? Phone, Bobby Lee! Get us to a phone!"

His telephone was ringing, but McCoy ignored it as he continued to watch the television screen. Bernard Shaw with the Atlanta station was saying, ". . . the State Department has just confirmed that an ATW airliner en route from Athens to Rome and New York was hijacked by unidentified terrorists a short while ago . . ."

The phone stopped ringing. The television coverage shifted to some dipshit reporter who, while backdropped by the Capitol Building, elaborated on how he didn't know anything more than anybody else in the dipshit District of Columbia.

The phone started up again. Grumbling, he picked it up. "McCoy."

The caller said, "Pope in one hour." Then he hung up.

McCoy sat staring at the glass debris in his fireplace. He rubbed the receiver across his eyebrows several times, then hurled it across the den.

The caller had been Nick Alexander.

7

1020 Hours . . . Over the Aegean Sea

"Wait here a moment . . . please," Gretti Werner said to the string of first-class passengers she had been leading back toward the tourist cabin. Behind her she could hear the one who called himself Colonel Abdul shouting instructions to Captain Campbell. And from the tail of the plane, the second terrorist, a boy with the broad face of a peasant, was strutting down the aisle toward her, striking heads he felt were not low enough with the stock of his submachine gun as he came.

Then he was standing before her, leering angrily. "What are you doing?"

"Your commander has ordered all the first-class passengers into tourist." She hesitated, but then found that she had to speak, she who as a child had chastised the neighborhood butcher for kicking his nervous little dog. For an instant her eyes were once again filled with the sight of that bloodstained apron as big as a sail. "Why are you beating them? They are doing what you say."

She knew by his silence that he was contemplating some kind of punishment for her, but at that moment Abdul elbowed his way down the line of first-class passengers and demanded, "What is the problem here? Mustafa—"

"This woman does not knowing how to—"

"Colonel Abdul," Gretti interrupted, gesturing at completely filled rows all the way back to the aft section, "where are these people going to sit?"

"They can share seats with the others."

"But that is not safe. If we should come into some turbulence—"

"Hurry up! In the back!" Abdul turned on the passengers, batted a tightly clutched purse out of a woman's grasp. "And leave your belongings here!"

Quickly, Gretti took the woman's hand and pulled her away from the terrorists, down the aisle toward the rearmost seating. In their fear the tourist-class passengers refused to meet her eyes—as if by accepting this refugee from first class they might, for some reason, be singled out.

"Excuse me," Gretti said to a Roman Catholic nun, whose eyes were friendly behind her gold-rimmed glasses. "We are asking you to share your seats. These men say they need the first-class cabin."

"Of course, dear." The nun gestured for the woman passenger to sit on her lap.

"Send another," the priest said.

"What do you mean?" the young man with a Russian accent asked. "Where? There will be no space to breathe here!"

Gretti ignored him and hurried back toward the rest of the first-class people, who had been delayed by Mustafa. The terrorist was shaking a man by the shirtfront—the young father who had already been so viciously pistol-whipped.

When Gretti tried to intervene, Mustafa swiveled his submachine gun on her. "I cut you apart!" he screamed.

She stepped back. Her hand gravitated to her throat.

Behind Mustafa, incredibly, Colonel Abdul was sitting on his heels, talking to a small girl. "So your name is Ellen. What does it mean?"

"I don't know," she answered in a tiny voice.

"Oh, it must mean something. Abdullah means 'servant to God.' Mustafa means 'chosen.' Chosen by God to do wonderful things." Reaching out to brush the soft curls around her ears with the hand that still clutched a grenade, Abdul took his lower lip between his front teeth for a moment. "Well, my Ellen, you may go back and get your doll. I have no use for a doll. I have no daughter."

As the child broke free of her mother's grasp and scampered back to retrieve the Cabbage Patch doll Gretti had made a fuss over earlier, Abdul glanced up and smiled warmly at the purser. Years ago, while in the cool and verdant park along the Isar River, she had looked back toward the heart of Munich just in time to see the setting sun glint spectacularly off the copper-clad dome of a church. It had given her a thrilling feeling of hope. And now Abdul's sad smile gave her the same sensation.

Perhaps they are human beings after all, she half prayed, half wondered. *Perhaps they will recognize their own brutality before it is too late.*

But then a grim-faced Abdul jerked his head for everyone to keep moving. "Hurry!" he barked, looking at Gretti. "All of you! Hurry!" He drove the passengers aftward as if they were sheep, kicking the last man in the rump whenever the line slowed. "Pull the shades!" he ordered everyone. "All the shades—down!"

In seconds the pale blue Mediterranean sky was shut out. Gretti's spirits dimmed with the sudden loss of daylight, but she forced a smile on her lips and shared it with everyone who met her eyes.

"Abdul!" Mustafa hollered from the first-class cabin.

"Come." Abdul motioned for Gretti to follow as he trotted up the aisle.

"Look!" Mustafa said triumphantly, his submachine gun clamped under his arm and the rifled contents of a purse on the carpet around his badly scuffed shoes. He was holding up an inscribed ring. "The words—they are in *Hebrew!* There are Jews aboard." He glared at Gretti. "You must be identifying these people for us!"

"I don't know who is Jewish and who isn't. How could I know?"

"Jews—yes, it may be a hard thing," Abdul said evenly. "But, as for Israelis, there is a way." He laughed, then shouted toward the main cabin, "Israelis—we are coming for you now!" Still laughing, he said to Gretti, "Collect all passports."

"Why?"

"Do it," he said in a low voice that made her glance at the unprimed grenade.

As if of its own accord, her hand reached for the intercom phone. She smiled, knowing that somehow, magically, a smile was projected in the voice. It was her duty as much as the captain's not to betray the slightest trace of fear, although for the first time in her life, she perfectly understood why her mother had never been able to discuss the wartime bombings.

"Ladies and gentlemen. This is your purser, Gretti Werner. I am sorry, but they require your passports. Please take them out and hold them over your heads."

Then she motioned for Tina Phillips, who had been sitting silently in her rear-facing stewardess's seat, to help her collect the documents. "Oh, God," the young woman whispered.

Gretti had just returned to the tourist cabin after shuttling her second ungainly load of folders to Abdul when she saw one passenger wedged in among three others kneading his passport with his thumbs. Clearly, he didn't want to part with it.

"Please, sir . . ."

She did not understand his reluctance. The passport bore a gold-embossed American eagle like most of the others she had gathered.

"Sir?"

"Benjamin," a woman, obviously his wife, whispered, "for the love of your children . . ."

All at once a defiant expression crossed the man's

otherwise gentle-looking, wrinkled face. With deliberate motions, he drew back his sweat-soaked shirt-sleeve, then the silver flex-band of his wristwatch—and revealed a crudely tattooed number.

Once Gretti had seen it, he hid the tattoo again and surrendered his passport.

"Let's just remember," Tom Hale said quietly to his fellow Marines, "the secret to staying alive is not to stand out. Blend in. Don't make too much or too little eye contact with them. We've been trained to survive this kind of shit."

"Aye, aye," Andy said in a hush.

Ed just winked.

Although he put on a good front for the sake of the others, Tom's own words seemed hollow to him. He knew what the terrorists would seek out among their 150 helpless victims: the epitome of what they despised, the perfect symbol for their rage. Ed was as solid a Marine as Chesty Puller, but he had Third World looks, and the terrorists might try to play off his being black. And Andy, frankly, was innocuous looking.

No, with blond hair, blue eyes and a square jawline, Tom knew who best fit the bill as the all-American boy. One of The Few. The Proud. The Terminably Visible.

He blew air out of his cheeks.

Young Jay, from the depths of a stunned quiet, kept peeking at him from across the aisle. He sneaked the boy a thumbs-up sign. But it did no good. Tom tried to say with his smile: *Kid, I'd love to fix bayonet and charge up this aisle at those miserable sons of bitches—just like I learned at Pendleton, barking like a devil dog, thrashing through the wild anise plants that gave off a licorice smell when you trampled them under your Nam boots.* Tom stared down at his useless hands. He knew that with one burst of automatic fire the interior of this aircraft might decompress like someone had pulled the plug on a black hole. A frag grenade or two would probably down this 727 —even if the fuselage didn't instantly vaporize into a fireball. And, if by some John Wayne miracle, he got to the first-class cabin and overpowered the bastards, what would it feel like to look back and see Jay slumped dead in his seat, his mother running her hands through his hair?

Shit, he fumed to himself, *I'm only eight hours and eight thousand miles away from being a student.* Away from wearing sweaters and Levi's instead of dress blues, cracking open books instead of crates of tear gas grenades, getting serious about a girl—now that he was finally free of the agreement he had made with the Corps not to marry while serving as a Marine security guard. All at once everything was on hold—perhaps for as long as 444 days, as was the case for the MSGs in Tehran—all because of some fanatics whose behavior was embarrassing to most Arabs.

Then Tom saw Andy go rigid in his aisle seat.

"Diplomatic passports!" the honcho, Abdul, screamed. "Who here has the diplomatic passports?" There was a new and frighteningly delirious tone to the man's voice. "Answer me! Answer or I kill!"

"Yo," Tom said firmly, slowly rising out of his seat.

"Are you all CIA? Tell me!"

"No," Andy said, unable to look away from the pistol barrel that was stuck in his face. "We're United States Marines. We have ID cards in addition to—"

"Filth!" Abdul tried to seize Andy by the top of his hair, but his regulation cut proved too short, so he pulled him out of his seat by the necktie and pressed the muzzle against the Marine's pronounced Adam's apple. "Come! All three of you! Come!" Abdul started walking backward, dragging Andy along with him. *"New Jersey? New Jersey?"* he was shrieking at them.

"No . . . Washington," Andy gasped.

Ed started to say Alabama, but the terrorist waved off his answer with the pistol. "No, no—the battleship!"

Tom didn't know how to respond. He certainly didn't want to admit to being an embassy Marine. "We aren't with the fleet. That's not our military occupation."

"Forward observers!" Abdul further accused them. "You were observers for the *New Jersey* in Beirut! You were the eyes for those guns!"

"No, man," Ed said, his attempt at a smile instantly becoming a grimace. "We've never been to Lebanon. None of us."

"We're en route back to our own country," Tom finally said. "We just finished a tour as guards at the embassy in Cairo."

They had reached the first-class cabin. Abdul said nothing for a moment. He wiped the sweat off the tip of his nose with the back of his hand. The other terrorist was squatting on the deck in a pile of discarded passports.

"Sit there," Abdul said, his rage spent. His pistol hand flopped to his side. "I have other business. Then I will decide whether or not to execute you for crimes against the Shia people."

0420 Hours . . . North Carolina

As he strode up the ramp of the black-skinned Hercules and entered its cavernous bowels, Peterson had a sudden fantasy that, like Jonah, he should be able to look around and see ribs and cartilage and a gullet as long as a Greyhound bus. But once inside he had no time to rubberneck: Bobby Lee and Doctor Jack were helping the Delta loadmaster secure one of the souped-up assault vehicles to the deck. Peterson lent a hand to a loader by steadying a cammy-green motorcycle while the pimple-faced kid tied it down. Two harmless-looking bread boxes were mounted to the rear of the machine's frame: 66mm multishot rocket launchers, accessories no serious biker should be without.

Jonah, he realized to himself, *for the second time in an hour the name Jonah has popped into my head.*

"Thanks, Sarn't Major." The loader rushed toward the next task on his checklist.

Do I really have a funny feeling about this one? Peterson couldn't decide. Maybe he always had a funny feeling before Delta was wheels up—and forgot the peculiar emotions of this moment in between operations. Maybe it was like having a baby—women claimed they couldn't remember the pain. Operation Eagle Claw—the aborted raid on Tehran. The assault on Richmond Hill Prison at Grenada. Both of those missions had certainly been like shitting a watermelon. *But how the hell did I feel before?*

Nancy hadn't helped when Bobby and he had let her off at her folks' place. Suddenly, with a voice that sliced through Peterson like a fléchette round, she cried from the amber-lit porch, "Pete!" It made Bobby Lee toe-dance on the brake pedal, and she came running through the flower beds to kiss Pete one more time. He had had to wave for Bobby to slowly pull away, or they'd still be there.

Staring out across the lowered cargo ramp, he could almost imagine that this was Da Nang, not Pope Air Force Base. Mist was hanging over the flight line—like it did sometimes between monsoon deluges.

Peterson smiled. *Hell, he'd come out of Vietnam all right.*

Doctor Jack was taking inventory inside his M5 medical bag, probably for the tenth time since his beeper had gone off. He was talking out of the side of his mouth to Bobby, who was swilling coffee directly out of a thermos when not gobbling down the medic's remedies for a hangover. "I'm in Washington anyways, Bobby Boy, so I decides to look Bethesda Hospital over. So, anyways, to make a long story short, I'm shooting the shit with this doper-looking Navy surgeon, see, and he asks me if we got a lot of short guys in Delta. Some, I guess, I says. And he says there's tons of dinky fuckers in the Marines—no offense intended, he says, on account of me being closer to pint than quart size. Anyways, he wants to do this study on what he calls the Little Guy Syndrome in the U.S. military. Well, I told him Walter Reed already done one. Oh, yeah? he asks, looking disappointed as hell he'd been scooped. Yeah, I says, and they found out that most short troops are short because their endocrinal secretions got diverted to their testicular regions during pubescent combat experience. And if it wasn't for ballsy little fuckers like me, big pricks like him would be working at the Josef Mengele Medical Institute, sewing twins together and collecting different colored eyeballs." Doc sighed, closing his bag. "So that's another thing I got going for me, Bobby —I been barred from the surgeons' lounge at Bethesda Naval Hospital."

Chuckling, Peterson went back down the ramp. If he really didn't put too fine a point on it, he probably felt happy deep down. If McCoy were here, he could really give in to the adrenaline rush all the other operators were savoring. He equated Scott McCoy with confidence. *But what the hell, nothing's ever perfect.*

There was a flash of silver from under the wing— Nick Alexander had removed his bonnie hat for a moment to smooth his hair. Although preflighting the Hercules was not one of his responsibilities, he was scrutinizing the condition of the plane, and from this Peterson knew that Desert One and its nightmare of mechanical failure was on the colonel's mind.

Yet when Peterson approached him, Alexander was wearing an ineffable smirk.

"Well, boss, thirty-five operators loaded and ready to roll."

"Thirty-six," Alexander muttered, running his eyes along the leading edge of the wing.

"Beg the colonel's pardon, I counted twice."

"About-face, Sarn't Major."

"Sir?"

"You heard me."

Peterson executed the command and stood at less than kosher attention, frowning, his gaze blearing on the window lights of the flight ops building in the distance. A figure was midway between the main doors and where Peterson waited for Alexander to finish playing this silly little game that was atypical for a colonel who called all the hired help by their first names.

Then his eyes snapped into focus on the approaching troop.

"McCoy!" Peterson cried. "You miserable mother-fucker!"

"That's *Major* Motherfucker to you, Sergeant."

"Yes, sir!"

"You really want to piss him off?" Alexander handed Peterson a fancy-looking packet of orders. Usually they came mimeographed and not gift wrapped like this set.

It was too dark to read the text, but the sergeant major couldn't mistake the Seal of the President of United States. "Sir?"

"It's a Presidential decree ordering him back to active service. Tell the stuck-up bastard he was shadowed by MPs all the way in from that rundown farm of his. They had orders to apprehend him if he did anything but drive straight here."

9

1135 Hours . . . Over Cyprus

Dave Hoskins, the flight engineer, asked in a whisper, "What did they want with all the passenger headphones?"

Gretti glanced back through the open cockpit door into the first-class cabin before answering. "There are three American soldiers aboard. The tubing of the phones was used to tie them to the first row of seats behind you." She then raised her voice. "Will you have more water, gentlemen?"

Each of the three men shook his head no.

"Purser!" Abdul snapped. "Come at once!"

"Be careful," Captain Campbell said, needlessly.

Abdul and Mustafa had been through the passports twice. The culls were heaped on the carpet around them. Sipping pineapple juice from a plastic cocktail glass, Abdul quietly asked Gretti if she would help him for a moment.

Once again his show of gentleness made her dizzy with hope. "Of course, Colonel Abdul."

"These"—he shook his pistol at the folders trashed on the deck—"they are nothing. And there are no Israeli passports among any of the 153 you so kindly collected for me."

Gretti wanted to throw back her head and shout for joy. But instead, she dipped her head downward, once.

"Now," Abdul went on in the same reasonable tone of voice. "The fact that these here . . ." He indicated a neat stack of perhaps twenty passports in one of the wide seats. All at once his gun seemed as inconsequential as a meerschaum pipe. ". . . were stamped by Israeli customs means nothing to us. Take this one . . ." He opened the topmost folder to the black-and-white photograph of the Roman

Catholic priest. "I doubt that he is a Jew, yes?"

Gretti tried to respond, but all at once she wanted to gag. Bile was worming up her throat.

"So we must rely on your help. Go through all the passports. Tell us which ones are Jewish names."

"What makes you think—?"

Abdul cut her short with a laugh. He said something to Mustafa in Arabic, who also laughed. Then Abdul asked her if she was in fact German-born, putting the question in barely understandable German.

"Yes," she said, refusing to speak anything but English, "but now I am an American citizen."

"*Nien—eine Deutsche!*" This must have exhausted Abdul's command of German, for he then resorted to English again. "I was a guest worker in Hamburg for six months long ago. I know Germans. And as far as a German finding Jews . . ." He laid his forefinger alongside his nose.

Finding the gesture obscene, she looked away, momentarily locking gazes with the blond American soldier. He tried to reassure her with a wink. Then she turned back to Abdul. "I will not do what you ask."

He blinked twice, then exploded. "What?"

"I cannot do this thing you ask."

"But you are a German!"

"Yes, and it is for that reason I cannot." Tears came to her eyes, but she felt nothing but anger. "Don't you understand? I am from Munich—where it all began. It is improper of you to—!"

She experienced the shock—but didn't understand what had caused it. The second blow she saw coming. Mustafa had thrown the punches, his fist fortified by the grenade he was clutching.

The blond soldier was screaming at the terrorists. He was doubled over, straining to break his bonds of headphone tubing.

Abdul kicked him in the face. Blood immediately

streamed out of his nose, and when he lifted his head again, enraged, he flecked red drops across the legs of the terrorists' slacks.

Gretti's own face was numb.

Abdul thrust the flat, cold end of his pistol between her eyes. She tried to focus on it, but stopped when she grew nauseous from looking cross-eyed.

"You will do this!" he bellowed, his pineapple-scented breath making her think, incongruously, of Waikiki, of big white clouds riding the trade winds over the hotel where she had stayed many times. "You will do this or I will shoot you!" He kicked a sheaf of passports against her folded legs. "Pick one up!"

Her cheekbones beginning to ache, she cracked open the folder. Abdul withdrew the pistol from her head. The name on the page above the photograph slowly swam into definition. "No," she said.

"Say it aloud for me."

"Rodriguez, Ernesto."

"Good. Now you have but 152 to go. This one next." He pressed the gun against her chest as she read. She closed her eyes.

"Well?" Abdul insisted.

Tears lined the lower lids of her eyes. She blinked them away.

"Say it aloud."

"Kaplan. Robert Kaplan."

"Is it a Jewish name?"

"I think so."

Abdul grinned. "Very good, my little purser. You are so smart I should marry you. The Kaplan I saw for myself departing from an El Al flight. You are alive because you did not lie to me. I respect you for that. We will soon ask Robert and Benjamin Kaplan to join us in this cabin." The grin vanished. Perhaps she had only imagined it.

"But you must tell little Ellen this is no great matter," Abdul said. "You must please do that for me."

Roger Campbell glanced from the distant, gray-green undulations of the Shouf Mountains to Colonel Abdul, who had taken up a post in the open cockpit door and now faced aftward, the purser's phone in one hand and a grenade in the other. The terrorist ordered Gretti to punch in the intercom so he might address the passengers. *Harangue the poor bastards was more like it,* Campbell thought. Eyes burning, the pilot turned forward again, noted the jutting contour of the Lebanese coast on which Beirut had existed with essentially the same name when Roman legionaries were hanging fanatics like this pair on crosses.

"Ladies and gentlemen," Abdul said breathily into the phone, "this is your new captain speaking . . ."

Campbell and his co-pilot, Jim Montgomery, traded uneasy glances. Dave Hoskins, the flight engineer, couldn't take his eyes off the tethered Marines in the first row.

". . . Colonel Abdul of the Musa al Sadr Brigade of Islamic Jihad. The words Islamic Jihad mean holy war, one waged by true believers against American-Zionist imperialism. Your purser will read some names out. If your name is called, come forward. If you do not come, I will blow up this plane and we will fall into the sea. I am sorry, but that is how it must be. We are all in the hands of God."

Through the corner of his eye, Campbell watched Gretti take the phone from her "new captain." The strain was making her look ten years older. He found himself wishing this were a deadhead run. With no passengers aboard, he'd love to give Gretti and the rest of his crew the high sign to strap themselves down. Then he'd dive so steeply the bastards would be pinned to the ceiling, so overwhelmed by Gs they'd be unable to scratch their noses let alone prime their grenades.

"Kaplan . . ." Gretti's voice was trembling. "Benjamin Kaplan."

"What are they doing?" Hoskins asked softly from his seat behind Montgomery. They had taken to communicating furtively through their press-to-talk microphones.

"Robert Kaplan . . . Harry Goldschmidt . . ."

Campbell whispered, "Separating the Jews from the others."

"Shit," Montgomery said, "like Entebbe."

Just the sound of the word threatened the back of Campbell's neck with gooseflesh. But if negotiations on the ground went to pot, or these idiots started killing passengers, armed rescue was what he might want more than anything in the world.

This was his first hijacking.

But he had lived with the specter of terrorism for a long time. There were things the public knew nothing about, like certain West German airports you left at a sharp-angle, full-throttle ascent, climbing as fast as you dared to put the three-thousand-meter effective range of a hand-held Soviet Sam-7 antiaircraft missile behind your tail—all because some boys and girls in an afterschool club called the Red Brigades had bought dozens of these toys at eighty dollars a copy on the French underground market.

But Campbell's risk-evaluative mind had accepted the potential for terrorism, just as he had learned to live with the threat of wind shear or an on-board fire. But the possibility—or the growing awareness that it was a *probability*—took its silent toll. He himself hadn't realized his own intensity of feeling about it until the news broke that *Grenzschutzgruppe 9*, West Germany's elite antiterrorist force, had given grenade-chuckers everywhere pause for reflection by flawlessly rescuing the hostages of an airliner forced down in Mogadishu. Campbell had phoned halfway around the world to wake up a Lufthansa pilot, an old drinking buddy from a dozen Oktoberfests, to shout, "Right on, Hans! *Wunderbar!*"

Now, as Gretti's quavering voice called out the name of Herbert Wechsler, he wondered if America's vaunted Delta Force was half as good as GSG-9. After all, while German proficiency was stereotypical, it was—in Campbell's experience—also true. And there was also the unsettling fact that Delta Force had never even made it into Tehran.

Gretti's voice welled up out of Campbell's thoughts: ". . . David Hoffman . . ." After a moment, she repeated the name.

Abdul seized the phone from her. "Hoffman—come forward or the blood of all is on your hands!"

"Please!" a cry came from the very rear of the tourist cabin. "I am not a Jew! Ask the priest! I am not a Jew!"

Campbell watched in horror as the one called Mustafa drummed down the aisle, directing his submachine gun on the place from which the offender's voice had sifted.

"Hoffman!" the terrorist bawled. "Where are you being from?"

The man rose, cringing. But then Abdul stepped into Campbell's line of sight, and the pilot faced forward, briefly closing his eyes during a scream of pain and then loud whimpering as David Hoffman was compelled to come to the first-class cabin.

"Time to put this bird on the ground," Campbell whispered. "Let's see how Colonel Abdul wants it done." But, turning to get Abdul's attention, he saw that both terrorists were confronting the Roman Catholic priest, who had also come forward.

"What is this?" Mustafa was shouting. "What meaning is this?"

"Your name was not called," Abdul told the priest. "Go back at once!"

"I heard my name," the priest said quietly.

A brave man, Campbell decided, because he could clearly tell that the portly clergyman was scared to death.

"That is impossible! You are not a Jew!"

"Today we are all Jews. Your violence makes us so."

"I kill him! I kill him, Abdullah!"

Campbell looked back in time to see Mustafa jam the muzzle of his submachine gun against the priest's neck.

"No!" Abdul pushed down the barrel. What happened next threw the priest completely off balance. Abdul warmly shook the cleric's hand as the latter looked close to fainting. "I see you want to be a martyr. I understand. I respect that. It is written that we true believers must honor those who also have a holy book. Do you have a Bible with you?"

"Yes . . . in the overhead compartment."

"You may go back and get it."

This seesawing between viciousness and kindness was wearing Campbell out. He would have almost preferred consistent terror. "Colonel Abdul—with your permission, I would like to contact the Beirut control tower."

"Of course," he said with infuriating reasonableness, sauntering into the cockpit and taking the empty observer's seat across from the flight engineer. "Can we land now?"

"Yes, as soon as the tower okays it."

"Which runway will you use?"

"Well, once again it's up to Beirut Control. But I'd like to use runway three-six."

"The one that runs the same way as the beach?"

"Yes." Campbell had been briefed that use of the only other runway entailed flying over the Burj al Barajinah refugee camp—and that was an invitation to taking a few rounds of small-arms fire from bored militiamen with nothing better to do.

Abdul chewed on his thumbnail, then waved impatiently for Campbell to go ahead. "Make it so I may hear."

The pilot turned on the cockpit speaker. "Beirut Control, this is ATW 827 . . . under the command of Colonel

Abdul of the Islamic Jihad organization. I am requesting landing instructions."

After several seconds of nothing but static, Beirut responded, "Flight 827, I am unable to give you landing instructions."

"Repeat, please."

"Unable to give you instructions. By order of the government, this airport is today closed to all international flights. Please do not land."

Campbell had a shocked grin. "Beirut, I've got a *situation* here. Do you understand me?"

Silence.

Abdul wiped his eyes with his coat sleeve. "What madness is the Phalangist government up to!" He grasped Campbell's shoulder. "Can you fly over the airport?"

"It might be a good idea. I have no idea what he means by *closed.*" Campbell hit the passenger cabin SEAT BELT and NO SMOKING sign switches, then banked over the lake-smooth Mediterranean and approached the city from the northwest, crossing the shore at the American University and following the line of artillery-damaged high rises along the once Riviera-like Ramlet el Baida beach toward the airport.

Abdul had risen and was leaning over Campbell, peering out the side window, tapping his grenade against the glass. He smelled strongly of nervous sweat.

"Look!" he cried, seizing Campbell by the forelock and yanking his face aside.

Momentarily, Campbell enjoyed a hopeful illusion that he was making the approach into Los Angeles International—here were the scrub-covered mountains, the California-style apartment buildings, the Pacific on two sides—but then he saw the tanks and buses blocking the runways on both sides of the main terminal complex, which also housed the obstinate control tower. And he knew then that he was making a flyby of the new hellhole of the Middle East.

"Talk to them!" Abdul's knuckles had gone white around the grenade.

"Beirut, the hijackers insist on landing at your airport. I am not in command of this aircraft. Repeat—I am not in command. Clear a runway or we've got a lot of dead people. Respond, please."

"I am most sorry, ATW. You do not have permission to land. This is final."

Abdul removed the pin. Bitterly, Campbell recalled the hopes he had entertained when the terrorist had replaced it after his initial show of force in the cockpit.

"Beirut, the hijacker has pulled the pin on his grenade. I have a grenade ready to go in the cockpit. This is a filled 727. I have no empty seats. One hundred and fifty plus aboard. Women and children . . ." Campbell paused to control his voice. A sob had come close to escaping his mouth. "Give me runway three-six, Beirut."

A new and more sympathetic-sounding voice came over the cockpit speaker: "Captain, this is Iqbal Ibn Suleiman, acting minister of defense of the coalition government. We do indeed understand your situation. But if these people elect to commit suicide, they must do it somewhere else."

"The Sunni dog!" Abdul screamed. "He who bought his way into politics by selling hashish! Tell him we will crash into the Knesset! The main gate to Atlit Prison— where the Zionists hold our brothers!"

"Which is it?" Campbell asked, struggling to keep his voice level.

But Abdul, who had taken a rushing stride toward the first-class cabin, suddenly halted, then asked, "Will a microphone go through the door?"

"No . . . I mean, I don't think so." Campbell turned to his flight engineer. "Give him your headset, Dave."

Abdul quickly stretched out the cord to its maximum length, but still it did not reach into the first-class cabin. Grunting, he aimed the mike in the direction of the blond

Marine, whose eyes flickered back and forth in anticipation of he knew not what, mucus trickling out of a blood-encrusted nostril.

"Press your button in there, Captain!"

"You're on the air."

Then Abdul said to his comrade, "Now."

Mustafa butt-stroked the Marine across the jaw with the submachine gun.

"No!" Abdul protested. "You will break it!" He handed the headset to Gretti and after a third savage kick, managed to wrench the armrest off a seat assembly. "Here! And Mustafa—do not knock him out. Just enough for pain." He took possession of the mike again and nodded for Campbell to key it from the console.

Mustafa put down his weapon, wound up a swing and delivered a bone-breaking blow to the Marine's shoulder with the armrest.

The young man screamed.

Abdul nodded approvingly. "Again."

The next strike surely snapped the Marine's clavicle. There was plenty of gurgling noise for the benefit of the acting minister of defense as the young man vomited into his own lap.

Beaming, Abdul gestured for the pilot to turn off the microphone. It took a moment for Campbell's trembling hand to find the switch. He was glad that Montgomery was flying the plane with fierce resolution, hearing nothing, seeing nothing but the horizon and the instruments.

"Captain?" Minister Iqbal was asking. "Captain, what is occurring there? Answer me, if you can."

"They're beating a boy to death . . . clubbing him to death. For the love of almighty God, give me a runway."

Waiting for a clearance he sensed would never come, slumping forward in his seat as if he himself had just been beaten, Campbell fixed his eyes on Mount Hermon rising out of the southeast, still laced with snow on its northern slope. He prayed that no one would die on his flight. He prayed that this young Marine would not die.

"Very well, Flight 827," the Beirut controller said, with the acting minister murmuring in the background. "You will be cleared to land runway three-six shortly. But await final clearance. And land quietly. Please land very quietly."

1700 Hours . . . Over the Mediterranean

McCoy was sprawled out in the troop seating area of the Hercules, listening to Bobby Lee prattle to Winnemucca, an operator from northern Nevada who was also a Paiute Indian. Winnemucca had broken down his M203, a dual-purpose weapon consisting of a 40mm grenade launcher under an M-16 rifle. He was caressing its sundry parts with a soft cloth, his intelligent eyes flitting now and again to Lee's mouth.

"All I want to know," Bobby drawled, "is why you spell your name W-a-u-k-e-n-e. Ain't it supposed to be Spanish, and don't Spaniards spell it—?"

All at once the coffee-brown hands were smoothly flying to reassemble the weapon. The task, as Bobby silently counted one-one thousand style, required all of a few seconds, including snapping the T-handle down and closing the bolt with the forward assist.

Smiling, his finger poised outside the trigger housing, Winnemucca whispered, "Boom-boom." He unleashed a trilled war whoop that reverberated inside the Hercules over the prop noise.

"Yeah, well, spelling never meant a rat's ass to me either," Bobby said.

"Major?" an operator called from the access steps to

the flight deck. "The boss would like to see you in the comm compartment, ASAP."

As soon as McCoy entered the cubicle, he checked the tracker graphics screen, which was being updated every fifteen seconds by satellite. The blue cursor blinking along the southern shore of Crete was the Delta Hercules. The red cursor—ATW Flight 827—was stationary on the central Lebanese coast. "Has it—?"

Alexander raised his hand, which had a Winston smoldering in it, and said to the technician beside him, "Put that window back on the screen for Scott, Teddy."

As soon as the inset appeared, McCoy knew that nothing had changed in the past several hours. "All right, she's still tied to the tarmac in Beirut."

"Affirmative."

"Are we cleared for a rescue?"

"I should know shortly. Sit down."

The screen went blank in the same instant an alert tone issued from the console speaker.

"Tell Major General Woodbridge who we are, Teddy."

The technician entered a code of at least twenty digits —McCoy stopped trying to count. Then the general's visage appeared on yet another screen that lit up directly across from Alexander's place on the console. A red lamp over a black plastic-rimmed lens indicated that Alexander was also on camera.

McCoy rolled his eyes at the colonel. "Do we go or not, sir?"

Alexander shushed him. "Hello, General—what's the verdict?"

As soon as Woodbridge touched a finger to his lower lip, McCoy knew that the operation was on hold.

"Nick, the President wants you to be ready to effect the rescue there at Beirut International. But . . . ." The general shrugged slightly.

"Here we go," McCoy said. "Tehran all over again."

". . . the President, on the advice of the National Security Advisor and key members of Congress, has decided to seek the approval of the Lebanese government before . . ."

"Oh, horseshit!" McCoy slammed his fist against the panel, making the general's image jump a frame. "Tell him the godamned PTA has more authority in Lebanon than Gemayel's government!"

"What was that, Nick?" Woodbridge asked. "We had some interference."

"It's being suggested here, sir, that it doesn't matter what the Lebanese government does one way or another. They exercise no real power. They couldn't figure in this even if they wanted to."

"That may be valid militarily, Nick—but not politically."

"Here we go," McCoy said. "Recipe for disaster coming up—four parts political to one part military."

"We can't hold Gemayel up as the legitimate leader of his country one day," Woodbridge went on, "and ride roughshod over him the next."

Alexander lit another cigarette, although one was still burning in his ashtray. "Well, sir, we're closing fast on Lebanon. What the hell do we do?"

"Proceed toward the airport. Our ambassador in Beirut promises a reply from Gemayel any minute. And we've also got feelers out to Hafez Assad to determine what Syria might do if we effect an armed intervention—"

McCoy shot up out of his chair but realized there was no place he could go.

"Very well, General. Just remind the President that waiting is what cost us a win in Iran." Then Alexander signed off. "Delta Force is standing by."

He averted McCoy's glare for a moment. "I don't like it any better than you do. But I'm a soldier. I do what I'm ordered to do. I suggest you do the same, Major." Alex-

53

ander turned to the technician. "Punch up that Beirut visual on the troop-bay screen for Major McCoy's briefing. I want us prepared to take a can opener to that 727 the second we receive a go-ahead."

‖

1730 Hours . . . Beirut

Abdul rested his chin on the back of the observer's seat. Mustafa had gone to keep watch in the sweltering tourist cabin. At least here in the cockpit, with the pilot's and co-pilot's side windows cracked open, a hint of breeze made the lack of air conditioning more bearable. The captain had tried to lie that the device that ran the air conditioner—the auxiliary power unit, he called it—used very little fuel, but it was obvious that he wanted to run down the tanks to delay another takeoff.

Fighting a growing heaviness in his eyelids, Abdul reminded the purser and the passengers in the first-class cabin with a languid brandish of his pistol that he had not forgotten them. The blond Marine's face was now so swollen even his own mother would pass by him in the marketplace. And the old Jew, who refused to look away like the others when singled out, was praying to himself.

Another cooling gust came through the pilot's window. A summer's late afternoon in Beirut. It almost seemed possible to walk home, to don a clean white caftan and retire to his small garden, to read from the Koran, to pause and hear his child's voice intertwined among other children's voices drifting over the wall from the shaded side street off Boulevard Saeb Salaam. But that home no longer existed; that garden grew only rubble.

Static crackled in the headphones. He sat upright. But no one in the control tower spoke to him.

Shaking off his drowsiness, Abdul rose and moved to the side window to have a look at the darkly tinted windows of the tower. As he did this, he was careful to keep his face close to Captain Campbell's and keep his pistol jammed into the nape of the man's neck in case Phalangist elements of the army had deployed snipers against him. Yet there was no activity to be seen anywhere around the terminal or at the line of trees on the bluff to the east.

An hour ago he had overcome his loathing for the acting minister of defense long enough to relate his demands to this Gemayel collaborator so that they might be passed on to the Americans. Now, after nudging the captain to activate the mike button, Abdul said, "Do not play games with me, Iqbal."

"The minister is away from the radio at present," a controller said.

"Summon him—at once." Abdul glanced around. The cockpit crew was beginning to stir out of their torpor. "Politics," he tried to joke, but they didn't laugh.

"Iqbal here."

"Yes," Abdul said, "I have waited long enough. What does the American President have to say?"

"Well, our representatives are still attempting to speak directly to him. But so far, it would seem, on the basis of statements made to us by the American Ambassador, that his government is reluctant to negotiate in any manner at all."

"Good, good." Abdul leaned out so Mustafa could see him, then signaled for the man to join him in the cockpit. "Very good then."

"I fail to see what can be good about this affair, Colonel Abdul," the minister said carefully.

"In five minutes I will shoot the first hostage. I will continue killing a hostage each five minutes until the hostages are no more. Please tell that to your reluctant American friends."

"Hold a moment—I beg you."

"I am holding, Minister . . . but only for five minutes."

The blond Marine had raised his face. His reddened eyes shouted at Abdul for a moment, but then his chin dropped against his chest again.

"Colonel Abdul," the familiar voice crackled in the earphones, "this is Georges . . . *Allah Akbar!*"

"*Allah Akbar,*" Abdul intoned automatically, perplexed why the man who had masterminded much of this holy mission, the Amal leader who was provisionally his superior, was rubbing elbows with the Maronite and Sunni hirelings of the Great Satan.

"Congratulations on your success. Our people are thrilled by your audacity. They shout your praises in the streets."

"All praise should be to God."

"Of course," Georges said, sounding a little less enthusiastic. "And now it is time to temper audacity with compassion."

"What do you mean?"

"Well, the world is watching, my brother . . ."

"Yes?"

"Abdul, we can gain much by being clever."

"I have never wished to be so. Jews, Sunnis are clever."

"That is true. But there are other, more important truths at stake." Georges's tone of voice had hardened.

He was a Shi'ite—but had come from a family of *beys,* big men who were accustomed to having their own way. He had come late to the cause, and only after Mossad, the Israeli CIA, had disrupted his profitable gunrunning business in southern Lebanon. French-educated, a wearer of gold chains and an expensive wristwatch, Georges did not have the proper spirit of a revolutionary.

He did not yet believe in the futility of political action.

"What are you proposing?" Abdul asked.

"Release the women and children."

"No! Never!"

"The Americans will enter into negotiations only if you do so."

"I do not care! Give me fuel or I will blow up this plane! I will leave Beirut! Yes, I will leave it for a . . . a friendlier place." His chest rising and falling steeply, Abdul peered out the cockpit windows again, looking for snipers.

"I understand, my brother," Georges said. "I understand completely."

Abdul was on the verge of shouting that he wished the entire operation had remained in the hands of Hizbollah, but then he remembered the insistence of the Syrians that that group not claim responsibility for fear Syrian positions would be bombed along with the Hizbollah headquarters in the Bekaa Valley. "I want to see a fuel truck *now*, Georges!"

"I have already given the order, my brother."

Abdul flopped back in the seat and dried his face with his sleeve.

"We are of the same cause, are we not, Abdul?"

"You make me wonder."

"You are weary, yes?"

Abdul shook his head, almost feebly. After the sleepless night while waiting in the Athens terminal and the taxing emotions of the last several hours, he felt close to exhaustion.

"It must be a near impossibility," Georges went on, "to keep an effective vigil on so many charges. And there is intelligence . . ." He let his voice trail off.

"Yes, yes—what intelligence?"

"The CIA may have operatives aboard."

Abdul glared down the aisle at the passengers. There were so many, and Mustafa and he were only two. In his heart he did not want George's militia more deeply involved. If the mission triumphed, Amal and not Hizbollah would receive the flood of zealous recruits. But Mustafa, sitting on the deck at the rear of the plane, looked very, very tired. And sometime in the next twenty-four hours, Abdul himself would have to sleep, even if only for a few minutes.

Abdul saw no other choice than to say, "Yes, Georges, it is almost too much."

The Amal leader understood at once. "And you will require food as well for your flight, yes?"

"Perhaps. But most of all we want fuel—so we may leave this place of decadence."

Strolling afterward down the aisle, Abdul paused at every tenth or so window and ordered the passenger sitting there to briefly open the shade so he could check on the progress of the small convoy approaching the 727 across the apron. It consisted of a food truck, a fuel pumper and a jeep manned by maintenance workers whose coveralls Abdul scrutinized carefully for suspicious bulges that might conceal weapons. The men appeared to be without firearms, nor did they carry themselves like soldiers.

He halted at the port rear service door and signaled for Mustafa to come to him.

An American passenger, more athletic looking than the norm, was staring at him. Abdul wondered if he might be one of the CIA people Georges had mentioned. Or perhaps it was all a trick by the Amal leader to have his way once again.

"What are you thinking?" Abdul asked the passenger.

The man said nothing.

"Are you waiting to be rescued by your United States Marines?"

The American shrugged slightly.

"Yes, of course you are. But let me tell you—I have three of these Marines up front, and they are worthless."

The purser was approaching without having been told to do so.

Abdul scowled at her. "What are you doing?"

"I saw the food truck coming. You'll need help opening the hatch."

"Very well . . . thank you, Miss Gretti." He turned to Mustafa. "Go inside the cockpit. Cover the fueling people with the Scorpion through the window that opens. Throw out a grenade and blow everything up if they try to deceive us."

Mustafa trotted forward, smacking a man's bald pate with his grenade as he went, leaving a bloody gash in the sunburned skin. The sight made Abdul smirk.

Gretti was facing the hatch, her face pale, her hands clasped before her.

"It is all a very bad dream, is it not?"

She looked up but didn't answer. Her eyes were very blue, quite pretty.

"Well, Miss Gretti, if all goes well, you will awaken from it in a few hours, a few days at most. Mustafa and I can never awaken. We were born to this nightmare, you see . . ." He suddenly inclined his head toward the hatch. There came a pneumatic whine from outside.

"The food compartment on the truck," Gretti explained. "It is on hydraulic lifters, risers."

Abdul raised his Beretta. "Open the hatch."

Immediately, a gush of sea breeze soughed around Abdul. He watched the aluminum box rise up to the level of the cabin. Quickly, he glanced behind to make sure the American passenger was still strapped in his seat. "Now, Miss Gretti, you will open the door to the box."

She no sooner touched her fingers to the latch than they surged out in a mass of dark clothing, their features hidden by black hoods, frenetic eyes flickering back and forth through holes in the head cloths.

A passenger hollered, "Everyone down—the Marines!"

Another American took up the same cry, but a Jew in the first-class cabin exulted, "Israelis! A rescue!"

So, Abdul realized, *each sees the intruders according to his own hopes and fears.* He alone saw the entry for what it genuinely was. He lowered his pistol as the twelve Shi-'ites filed past him to cow the murmuring passengers into silence with their Kalashnikov rifles. *Yes, my poor captives,* he chuckled to himself, *American Marines do not use Russian assault rifles. Nor do the Israelis.* This knowledge wiped the dazed joy off the faces of those captives who knew about such things. These men began whispering the disappointing news to the others.

Mustafa had appeared in the cockpit door, ready to open fire. But a greeting in Arabic made him suddenly jerk the snout of his Scorpion toward the ceiling. "Brothers!"

The commando standing nearest Abdul whipped off his black hood and grinned. The Amal lieutenant kissed Abdul on both cheeks.

Abdul returned the courtesy—but only perfunctorily. Amal was taking over in its typical milk-and-water fashion: by pulling on the donkey's nose and tail at the same time—both holding the prisoners and trying to arrange for their release.

Yet, Abdul reminded himself, *I still have a pistol, a grenade and absolutely no fear of dying. May that prove enough.*

Blackness. The utter absence of light that was death.

Benjamin Kaplan was jostled down the aisle by rude hands and prods from the barrels of rifles. His son, Robert, he thought to be in front of him, and the Negro Marine to his back. At least this is what a final glimpse had told him before the blindfold was secured tightly around his head.

The last time it had been his father before him and

his uncle behind him in line. And the guards had held Schmeissers.

Benjamin wanted to put distance between himself and the first-class cabin. He could hear his wife wailing as his daughter-in-law tried to comfort her. But it was not Edie's voice that was piercing him; it was his mother's.

Never again!—what a joke. Just an empty slogan like all the others he'd heard in his sixty-six years. For here it was again; the systematized fury, the growled orders, the creak and rattle of guns being shifted this way and that by fisted hands. Perhaps forty years of living in White Plains had been a delirium that attended the last stages of starvation, and he was still in Poland, lying in a bunk with the others he had only imagined to be long dead. *God forbid. Yes,* he decided, *that is much better than* Never Again. *It takes the inescapable helplessness of it all into account. God, please forbid . . .*

An Arab grasped his upper arm to make him halt. How he hated to be touched. Even Edie had to be careful sometimes how she touched him.

They were arguing among themselves now. A breeze was coming from somewhere.

"Wait—leave me one of the Marines."

"For what purpose, Colonel Abdul?"

"He may be of use."

"I would rather—"

"Leave one—that one. The fair-haired one. I order it as commander of this aircraft!"

"As you wish, Colonel Abdul. But Georges believes the Marines will have value for the negotiations here in Beirut."

"No, he will have value here. He more than any of the others questions the righteousness of our cause."

"Not your cause," the Marine said, his words thick from swollen lips. "It's your methods that suck."

Benjamin winced. The young man was being pummeled once again.

He had survived a hundred of these grim little vignettes and knew something that even the Marine did not know. If the animals chose to kill, it would be this young man they would slay first. An unconscious trait of his had already singled him out. Benjamin had seen the same quality bring death to a canter with a voice better than Caruso's, a nineteen-year-old Polish cavalry officer, a coal miner from Silesia, even a Gypsy horse trader. What was it? A natural dignity perhaps. But whatever it was, this effortless, God-given sense of self-worth reminded the animals what human refuse they were. It infuriated them. They had to murder it, or risk seeing themselves for what they truly were.

All at once Benjamin was fighting back tears. *I will remember.* He had even asked the purser for the Marine's name. "*I promise I will remember, Thomas Hale. Never will I make it easy on myself and forget.*"

Then Benjamin was being herded into some kind of wood-lined space. All it needed was the stench of urine to become the interior of a boxcar.

"Step back! Make room for more Jews!"

"Please do not hurt them!" the purser begged.

Although his tears were now flowing freely into the blindfold, Benjamin tried to smile in her direction. He prayed she saw it.

If he survived this, he must talk to the German girl. A misconception was costing her needless anguish, worsening a situation that was already impossible for her. Somehow she thought that in order to be a Nazi one had to be a German. Nonsense. He had known Nazis of all nationalities and races. And, sad beyond sad, he had even known Jews in the camps who were Nazis. All one needed to become a Nazi was the willingness—no, the *eagerness* —to shove a gun, a club, a fist in an innocent man's face and compel him to abandon God's most precious gift: hope.

He and the others were being forced across the tarmac now, their shoes scuffling along the ground. The sun was hot for this late in the day. The engines of the jet had begun to whistle.

"Inside! Bend low! Inside!"

He was shoved into some kind of van or truck, banging his knees on a running board as he fell forward, his fingers brushing another pair of tied hands as he hurried to draw in his legs, which were being kicked again and again by one of the Arabs.

"Dad?"

Benjamin grasped the hands he had just felt. They belonged to his son, Robert. "I'm fine."

Ten minutes later the vehicle began to move, making a noise as its gears were shifted very much like those of Benjamin's 1947 Chevrolet, the first car he had ever owned. "Forty years ago," he whispered to his son, "I went halfway around the globe to a strange country where I had no friends—to spare my children, my grandchildren this kind of thing."

"It isn't your doing."

"If only that were a comfort."

Suddenly the van was sharply braked, pitching Benjamin against a forward bench seat.

There was a roar, and he knew at once that Flight 827 had departed again.

"*Allah Akbar!*" his captors shouted in farewell to the plane.

"Lord God forbid," Benjamin said.

As the Hercules executed a slow ellipse time and again three hundred miles off the Levantine coast, protected by an aircap of F-14s off the carrier *Nimitz,* McCoy watched the mood of the Delta operators go from buoyant to indifferent and finally depressed—the last when the transport broke off the orbit and headed to Greece for refueling. Combat gear was stowed again as coffee brewed in the small galley.

Once more the wait was on.

And when the Hercules was airborne again and had cleared the Greek airspace, continuing westward over the Mediterranean, everybody, including McCoy, assumed the worst: the operation had been scrubbed. Flight 827 was headed for some country the President didn't want to tangle with, and the Delta was on its way back to a NATO facility in Sicily or even home to Fort Bragg after a stopover in Spain. *You don't keep doing this to an elite fighting team,* McCoy railed to himself in silence. *You don't lead them to the starting blocks, then cancel the race.*

Colonel Alexander was keeping to himself in the communications compartment. The hatch had been shut since Greece, and McCoy had no urge to go knock on it. He understood Nick's position. Alexander either obeyed orders or the modern breed of hacker-generals would put one of their own in his slot. He understood Woodbridge's position . . . somewhat. Hell, he even understood the President's position. But all this goddamned understanding wasn't putting a dent in the fact that one-third of all terrorist activities worldwide were being directed against citizens of the United States, a relatively small fraction of the earth's population. If you didn't like how things were run in your mud-and-wattle village, you kidnapped an American. If you were a Moslem and didn't like Jews, you said it with dynamite to the American Ambassador—who might be a Buddhist for all you knew.

Whatever your gripe, the motto was: Get an American.

It had to stop.

But nobody wanted to draw the line. They said it couldn't be done. And *they* were the anemic offspring of the same weak sisters who in 1940 counseled neutrality because Hitler couldn't be beat.

It could be stopped, and Scott McCoy was willing to bet his life on it.

A glimmer of hope arose when, instead of descending for a landing at Sigonella Air Base, the Hercules continued westward right over the top of Mount Aetna—so low McCoy could've pissed off the ramp into one of the volcano's smoking fumaroles. This Sicilian landmark was maybe 11,000 feet high, which meant the pilot hadn't ascended to the fuel-saving cruising altitude.

Peterson had sniffed something too, for he'd left the troop seating area and now joined McCoy at the window on the paratroop door just aft of the port wing. Both men looked down through the heat exhaust of the turboprops at the last hint of sunset over the North African coast.

"Tunisia maybe?" Peterson asked after a moment.

"Maybe. Or Algeria. Morocco."

The sergeant major was smiling. "It'll come together this time."

"You promise?"

"Promise."

An alert buzzer sent them forward again. They wended their way through the tie-downs for the assault vehicles and motorcycles, reaching the seating bay just as Alexander came drumming down the flight-deck access steps. When the colonel checked his watch, then looked right through half a dozen anxious operators as if they weren't there, McCoy guessed that Alexander was dividing airspeed by miles.

The colonel had an objective in mind.

Delta Force might have a purpose in life again.

"All right, listen up," the colonel shouted over the prop noise, "the bad news is that we lost our chance in Beirut."

"No shit," McCoy whispered.

"The flight departed for an unknown destination. But let me say this. For a while this afternoon, the pucker factor in both Washington and Jerusalem went to ten. One of the two hijackers believed aboard made a threat earlier to crash that bird into the Israeli parliament building. This is so classified I don't even know it—but that ATW pilot came within about five air miles of scrambling the rest of the Israeli Air Force that wasn't already shadowing him with Sidewinder missiles, waiting for him to even *think* of making a left bank."

"Question, boss," Bobby Lee said.

"Go."

"All that was hours ago. Where's the bird now?"

Alexander smirked. "Where would you go if you were Colonel Abdul of the Islamic Jihad?"

"Some friendly A-rab country, sir." Bobby scratched his chin. "Libya maybe."

"Well, Israeli military intelligence says we can scratch Muammar's place off our list. Seems these terrs are Lebanese Shi'ite Moslems. Eight years ago their head holy man, an *imam* named Musa al Sadr, went calling on Colonel Qaddafi. Just a social visit. But I guess Muammar didn't take a liking to Musa because he had him offed— then told the Shi'ites their man vanished inside his hotel."

"Yeah," Peterson said, "room service brought him a poached frag under glass."

Alexander waited for the dry chuckling to die away. "No, these particular Shi'ites are more apt to go to Iran than Libya. But they haven't done either. For whatever his reason, Colonel Abdul has apparently decided on another 'friendly A-rab country,' as Bobby says—one, incidentally, that's also friendly to us at the moment." Then he shouted through the open flight deck hatch: "Teddy—hit it!"

The unmistakable runway configuration of an airport appeared on the troop bay screen, although the data window was still blank. "Anybody?"

Winnemucca stood. "Houari Boumédienne International Airport, Algiers, Democratic and Popular Republic of Algeria, sir." He sat again.

"Bingo, Waukene." Alexander paused, squinting at the operator, who had gone back to scraping his survival knife across a small sharpening stone. "And I don't know how the fuck we beat you people."

"That makes two of us, boss."

Before the laughter was completely spent, Alexander went on, "So our Colonel Abdul broadcast a message at 1830 hours today that he will release his female and juvenile hostages if two things are done. One, Israel frees seven hundred Shi'ite POWs they've been holding to cover their asses while withdrawing from south Lebanon. Two, the Greek government releases one Jaffar Ibn Khalil, who screwed the pooch and never made it aboard in Athens. He's to be flown to Algeria and turned over to his pals, who presumably will be there also, waiting in an ATW Boeing 727 with our name on it."

"Question, sir."

"Shoot, Scott."

"Does this mean that we've already got a solid go on this caper?"

Alexander met McCoy's gaze for a long moment. "This means the Algerian government has cleared us to set up a covert operation at Algiers Airport. Final approval must come from our President."

13

As the ramp whined down out of its housing in the aft section of the Hercules, McCoy was surprised to see a thin fog blowing across the apron. The stuff was being backlit the color of champagne by the amber lights of the terminal building flickering from perhaps a half mile away across the main runway.

The transport would not remain at the airport during the operation, so McCoy and thirty-five operators who trotted out of the aircraft behind him had to brace themselves against the prop blast as they negotiated the thirty meters of slick tarmac to the side door of the abandoned hangar.

An Algerian soldier, sporting a crimson beret with a silvered insignia bigger than a Czarist decoration, directed the Americans inside, smartly waving his white-gloved hands like a traffic cop.

Letting the men file in first, McCoy had a parting glimpse of Colonel Alexander being whisked away by the Algerian brass in a chromium-blue Land-Rover, damp flags refusing to billow out from their fender mounts.

For a few seconds McCoy took stock of Houari Boumédienne International. He'd expected a desert ambiance, big stars hanging ten feet off the deck. But this was like Upper Peninsula weather in late spring. The misty conditions might help his operators approach the aircraft, but it would give fits to the snipers.

Inside the echoing chamber, he quickly took inventory and was pleasantly surprised, at first glance anyway, to see that the Algerians had put together everything Alexander had asked for: three Algerian Army jeeps, a fuel tanker truck, and two Red Crescent ambulances—the Islamic equivalent of the Red Cross.

Arrayed in neat rows on the oil-stained concrete floor were two styles of uniforms: airport maintenance and Algerian commando desert cammies, the latter disguise replete with *khaffiyeh* headgear, which the immaculate Algerian soldier was explaining in French how to don *avec panache*.

Peterson had brushed off his Viet French and was trying to translate these instructions to the nine operators of his section.

Most of the Delta operators would be passing themselves off as President Chadli Bendjedid's finest—purely for political reasons. If things went awry, the Algerians preferred it that the rest of the Arab world believed that they had brought the hammer down on the hijackers by their own volition and with their own troops. The last thing a country that was ninety-nine percent Moslem wanted was a jacket as a pawn of the American infidels.

Before slipping on his own less dashing pair of maintenance coveralls, McCoy took the two snipers aside. From an already elite group of fighters, these imperturbable-looking operators had been singled out for what Alexander and McCoy had recognized as the ability to maintain an exquisite emotional balance in the craw of an experience few men ever knew, let alone understood. For hours on end, for days even, they might have to peer at a man through a scope—watch him eat, drink, laugh, despair—and then marshal the objectivity to put a bullet in his head when the time came.

"We're going to do a little quick improvising," McCoy said to them. Ordinarily, one of them did the sniping, the other the observing, and a third operator saw to it that nothing disturbed their concentration. "With this haze and damned little high ground to work from, I want both of you with Remingtons in your hands. It's going to be tough enough to get a shot." He looked at the Algerian, who was grinning at them while listening to Peterson, who was brushing up on his Arabic. "Play it like *everybody* here's a hostile."

"You bet, little boss."

"Matter of fact . . . Winnemucca!"

"Yo!" The operator came jogging over in Algerian uniform, his M203 slung over his shoulder.

"I want you to watch their backs, Waukene."

The operator shrugged as if that was fine with him. McCoy smiled. "You loaded for bear?"

He produced one of the gold and green 40mm high-explosive rounds. It was capable of penetrating two inches of armor plate and chew a five-meter swathe out of an infantry assault. "Loaded for *grizzly.*"

"Good luck. Give me some fresh call signs for to-night."

Winnemucca rolled his tongue along the inside of his cheek. "How about Zap One, Two and Three?"

"Consider yourselves christened. We've got a moon-rise in an hour. Go." McCoy watched them depart, then stepped into his coveralls and pulled them up over his dark jump suit and body harness.

It occurred to him that he really believed in these people. And he wouldn't hesitate to match their perform-ance level against any counterterrorist organization in the world. In the formative stages of Delta, Alexander and he had trained with Britain's Special Air Service and West Germany's *Grezschutzgruppe* 9. Both were outstanding outfits, but much of each group's methodology was intrin-sic to its national character. Nick and he had soon realized that SAS, GSG-9 or even the underrated Italian C-T unit could not be replicated with an American roster. At eight years of age, Waukene Winnemucca had been able to pop the eye out of a streaking Nevada jackrabbit with an octa-gon-barreled .22 at one hundred meters, but it took an act of Congress and a personal plea from the Joint Chiefs to get him to spit-shine his boots. Bobby Lee was on a first-name basis with every radar-equipped state trooper in North Carolina, although he talked so slow he sometimes seemed retarded—yet, when everything was at its worst, he was invariably at the right place doing the right thing.

Delta didn't always do it like clockwork, and it never did it pretty. But if a precisely planned operation suddenly few apart, and most operations had a habit of doing that, McCoy wanted to be with *these* people. He was positive they had an untested genius for tinkering with disaster and turning it into success.

Nick Alexander's Algerian counterpart, a young colonel with handlebar mustaches, wasn't exactly chummy. A Moslem no doubt, he probably thought his government was backing the wrong side tonight. But orders were orders. Frowning, he reached across the arms of the middle-aged driver to activate the wipers for a few strokes. The air was just soupy enough to scum up the windshield after a minute or two.

The driver apologized in French for his inattentiveness.

The colonel grunted something in Arabic.

Alexander smiled: the modern history of Algeria in two sentences.

Immediately upon entering the Land-Rover, he had been handed a portable monitor so he could listen to the control tower's radio traffic. He also carried in his leg pocket a Delta tactical transceiver, $20,000 worth of sophisticated, satellite-interfacing communications he could hold in one hand—but he wouldn't fire it up until he had some privacy. Woodbridge wanted *no one* to know about the capabilities of this miniature unit.

Red dots trickled across the face of the Algerian monitor without pause; so far, no more words of revolutionary wisdom from Flight 827, which the colonel explained had been put in a holding pattern an hour ago, ostensibly to coordinate its arrival with that of the Olympic Airways jet carrying the hapless Shi'ite who'd been napped in Athens. The Algerians had told the head hijacker that they wanted a smooth transfer with the ATW 727 on the ground "as briefly and expeditiously as possible."

For once Alexander felt like he was being treated to an overhead view of the Maze. The Beirut Humint, or human intelligence on the ground, had it that the two hijackers were close to exhaustion—Colonel Abdul had quarreled bitterly with his possible superior, who had suffered a lapse in fervor and advocated negotiating with the Great Satan. Humint also had it that the bastards aboard were slowly beating a Marine lance corporal to death.

Sitting in the communications compartment aboard the Hercules all those long hours, Alexander had debated whether or not to share this last bit of intelligence with his operators. Finally, he decided no. They were already frustrated, and should the operation have to be aborted again, this report would only add rage to that frustration.

But things looked good. Better than perfect for taking down a pair of weary terrs with more than 150 wards on their hands. Alexander smiled to himself, reaching for a Winston. Still grim-faced, the Algerian officer nevertheless insisted that the American help himself to a cigarette from the gold case he snapped open.

Alexander lit up and suppressed a cough. He was trying to think of the Arabic word for dogshit when the monitor crackled to life.

"Algiers . . . this is Flight 827." The pilot's voice was raw with fatigue. "Colonel Abdul demands that we now land . . ." What came next almost sounded like an afterthought. ". . . or he will blow up this aircraft. We will await Olympic Airways on the ground. We can't hold any longer."

The Algerian colonel looked to Alexander, who gave him a terse nod.

"Tower," he said, keying the mike to the Land-Rover's Motorola, "this is Colonel Aziz. You may give him landing instructions for runway one-two. He is forbidden to taxi up to the terminal. This is for his own security. Tell him he will be directed."

"Very good, sir."

"And you may put our negotiator in communication with Colonel Abdul again. It is time to press for the release of the women and children."

The driver breezed through a cordon of Algerian troops around the terminal building and parked near a utility entrance manned by two sentries, who came to plebe-perfect attention.

"This way, please, Colonel Alexander." Colonel Aziz had dug up a tiny smile for the first time. He steered Alexander by the elbow into elevator that eased them up two stories and delivered them to a large suite with plush maroon carpeting and ultramodern furniture—all glass and chrome. There were a lot of Arabs dressed like Englishmen standing around, sipping tea and nibbling on crackers with caviar. A few of them could not conceal their disdain at the sight of Alexander's camouflaged jump suit and faded, twenty-year-old boonie hat he wore whenever away from Fort Bragg.

The tower traffic interrupted the Muzak coming over speakers in the ceiling. Everyone looked up.

"Flight 827," the controller asked, "do you see our man?"

"Roger."

"Kindly obey his parking directions."

"Roger."

Ignoring the offered hand of a U.S. envoy, Alexander asked Colonel Aziz, "Where can I get a view of the plane?"

"Follow me."

He was led out to a balcony, a good vantage from which to view the operation—especially now that the breeze was picking up and the fog becoming sparser.

The first thing Alexander noted through his binoculars was that the passenger windows were blacked out. The screens had been pulled down. He could not see the pilot's windscreen from here. As intended, the cockpit was pointed toward the hazy darkness and not into the terminal lights, which would only serve to silhouette the Delta operators for the hijackers.

"Flight 827, this is Hassan," a silky voice said over the monitor. "I would like very much to speak to Colonel Abdul of the Musa al Sadr Brigade of Islamic Jihad."

"One moment," the pilot said.

"Yes, yes—this is Colonel Abdul," the hijacker said crossly.

Alexander smirked. The man was bone-weary. His voice was as thin as October ice.

The Algerian hijacker went on, "Your comrade, Jaffar Ibn Khalil, has just touched down."

"Good . . . that is good."

"So now, my brother, will you give the world what you have promised?"

"What of the Israelis?"

"They have released seventy of your brothers who, at this hour, are on their way home."

"That is but a tenth of our . . . our hostages at Atlit Prison."

"My brother, please—the united Arab community is heartened by this gesture."

"I will be heartened when all seven hundred are freed."

"Please, Colonel Abdul, will you consider what is written?"

A moment of wordless static. Abdul had keyed his mike, then released the button without speaking.

"Brother," the negotiator went on, "is it not written: *As for helpless men, women, and children who have neither the strength nor the means to escape, Allah may pardon them. He is benign and forgiving . . . ?*"

Silence from the plane.

"Abdul, my friend, do you hear these holy words?"

"I hear. I will decide when Jaffar is once again with us."

Nick Alexander caught Colonel Aziz's eye. "If you'll excuse me for a few minutes."

The Algerian gave him the same curt smile as before and withdrew.

Alexander removed the transceiver from his leg pocket and turned it on. He now had three frequencies at his disposal: one linking him to his operators, one to Teddy at the console aboard the HC-130, and one to Woodbridge at the Pentagon.

Sitting behind the wheel of the fuel tanker, Scott McCoy concealed the lightweight headset of his transceiver under his ATW baseball cap, then adjusted the wire-thin boom mike until it rested an inch below his bottom lip. "Section One to any Zap unit."

"Section One, go from Zap One."

"You comfy yet?"

"As comfy as you can get on top of a Gooney."

"Copy." McCoy sat back. His first sniper was in place on a C-47 he'd spied earlier parked across the runway. The operator was probably sprawled out on a wing. Hopefully, Zap Two had found a higher position than his partner's, although the antique aircraft was less than two hundred meters from where Flight 827 would come to rest.

"Section One," the same sniper said, "here comes our bird. I got landing lamps coming out of east southeast."

McCoy related the sighting to the others in his section. Peterson and Bobby Lee, who as section leaders were equipped with their own transceivers, gave the word to their men.

And everyone in Delta Force fell silent, listening beyond the curved ceiling of the hangar for the throaty harmonizing of three Pratt & Whitney turbofan engines.

Bobby Lee and Doctor Jack, each in the driver's seat of an ambulance, leaned their heads outside their open windows and looked upward.

The second sniper said in the same instant that McCoy first heard the roar, "Confirming an ATW 727-200, Section One."

McCoy saw that Peterson, looking like Lawrence of Arabia in the Algerian commando getup, was grinning at him. "You promised," he mouthed the words during the blaring arrival of the jet through the thick, moist air.

Peterson gave him a thumbs-up.

"Section One, I've got another set of landing lights in the east."

That would be the Greek airliner bringing the third terrorist to the biggest surprise of his twenty-one years.

"Any Zap unit," McCoy asked, "can you see inside the cockpit of Flight 827?"

"Zap One—negative. The plane's taxiing away from me now."

"Affirmative from Zap Two. Through the eyebrow windows I see the top of the co-pilot's head. I see the pilot waist up. No hostiles in view. I'm losing my visual on the cockpit now. The dummy with the flashlight is missing the mark we gave him by a hundred meters."

"Fucking figures," McCoy muttered without keying his mike.

Colonel Alexander broke in. "Go to Tac Two, Major."

McCoy switched channels. "McCoy here."

"All right, we've got a green light to roll—with one hitch. There's a chance the Algerians can trade that Jaffar joker for all the women and children aboard. And, Scott, the President thinks that would be a pretty good swap from a tactical point of view. So do I."

McCoy rubbed his forehead with his fingertips. "Okay, Nick—me too. Let's just not wait too long. The window on this chance is going slam shut before we know what happened."

"You know it. Get your people deployed."

McCoy tapped the fuel truck horn twice, and the Algerian soldier rolled open the hangar door. The operators of Pete's section jumped onto the truck's running board, and Delta Force convoyed out into the misty night toward Flight 827.

14

2220 Hours . . . Algiers

Leaving Mustafa to guard the crew in the cockpit, Abdul raced down the aisle, collaring Amal militiamen as he went and pointing out places of concealment to them. "There, brother, and do not stand unless it is to return fire."

As an extra precaution, he hid a gunman in the galley at the front of the plane and one in each of the rear lavatories.

Then, grasping the purser by the wrist, he asked, "You must tell me, Miss Gretti—how may one get on the airplane without the use of a ramp? I will not permit them to connect a ramp to this plane."

She closed her eyelids for a moment.

"Tell me!"

Her eyes startled open. "The rear ventral airstairs . . . can be lowered."

"Can you operate them?"

"Yes."

"Excellent . . . I did not mean to shout so." He patted the hand he had seized, then released it.

"What will happen now, Colonel Abdul?"

"You will see. You will see, my friend."

The Beretta had ridden up in his waistband, and he now tucked it down again as he hurried back into the cockpit, closing the door behind him. On the way he had glimpsed little Ellen sleeping in her mother's arms. He had wanted to wake her to tell her the excellent news, but then he quickly realized that she would not understand. One that small understood so little—which was a blessing, he felt sure.

He peered through the windscreen, but saw nothing but the grayness of an overcast night, the faint glow in the east of the moon, which, on the brink of rising, was casting a delicate fog-bow around the tail of an old airplane parked on a distant apron.

"From this moment on," he told Captain Campbell, "this door is to remain shut."

"Okay."

"And as soon as we have refueled, you must be ready to start the engines again. We must be prepared to go whenever I say."

"Colonel, my crew and I are beyond the point of being able to safely fly this aircraft. We need rest."

Abdul held up a hand for the pilot to be quiet—but he did not strike him. By now he was proficient with the various communications controls. He put on the headset and reached over the pilot's shoulder to key the microphone. He demanded to speak to Hassan.

The negotiator immediately said, "Yes, my brother?"

"So be it—I will let the women and children go as soon as Jaffar is brought to this plane."

"*Allah Akbar.*" Hassan suddenly sounded as if he were on the verge of weeping. "He is on the way . . . You have shown greatness this hour."

Abdul piped his own tremulous voice into the cabins. "Ladies and gentlemen, I have excellent humanitarian news for you. Islamic Jihad has agreed to release all women and children on this flight."

The sounds of cheering sifted through the closed cockpit door.

"Thank you, Abdul," Captain Campbell said, trying to smile through his exhaustion.

"When you leave," Abdul continued to the passengers, "it is necessary that you leave behind all money and jewelry. These are lawful reparations for the crimes your government has committed against the Shi'ite Nation."

Mustafa looked confused. "Is it wise to let them go? Israel has not freed all our people, Abdul—"

"That is coming. They are weakening in the face of our resolve."

"It would seem that *we* are showing weakness by—"

But Abdul brushed past him and hurried out the cockpit door, waving impatiently for Gretti to approach him. "Quickly, where is that slide thing?"

She pointed behind him at a pack attached to the front entry door. "There—it's called the escape chute."

"You know how to work it, yes?"

"Yes."

"Very well . . . come with me now." Sidestepping through the first-class cabin, he paused to pat the blond Marine's shoulder almost affectionately. One of the American's eyes was swollen completely shut, and the other was narrowed to a red-lined slit.

He looked up at Abdul, befuddled, perhaps not seeing anything but the bloody tint of his own iris.

Smiling, Abdul worked his way along the rows, reassuring the Jewish women that their husbands and sons were being well cared for "somewhere" in Lebanon. Was not Arab hospitality famous? He kissed the tips of two fingers, then applied them to the soft cheek of the sleeping child. "You must say good-bye to her for me."

Ellen's mother only glared in reply.

Reaching the port rear door, he gave Gretti a wink, then peered outside, showing only a sliver of his face. He laughed. "Come, Miss Gretti—have a look."

Her eyes widened as she stared down onto the tarmac.

"What do you see, woman?"

"A white Mercedes. People still inside. A shuttle bus is coming now. A big banner on its sides." She looked to Abdul. "In Arabic?"

He peeked out again for only an instant. "Yes. The first one declares: *Say unto the infidels, do whatever lies within your power and so shall we.*"

"From the Koran?"

His eyes softened as he nodded yes. "You are a brave woman."

She gazed outside again. "A young man is getting out of the Mercedes. He is walking this way."

"What about the men with him?"

"No, they are staying in the car."

"Do you see any soldiers? Any men with guns?"

"No . . . a fuel truck coming . . . the old tanker kind . . . and behind it some ambulances."

Abdul chuckled. "What is the young man doing?"

"He is waving for me to open this door."

"This morning I cared nothing if I ever saw him again. But now it will gladden my heart to embrace him. Let down the back stairs for my brother, Miss Gretti."

McCoy rested his chin on the crown of the steering wheel, doing his best to look slightly bored as he waited for the last stewardess, the purser, if rank meant anything to the airlines, to come careening down the vinyl chute from the front port entry into the waiting arms of two Algerian government officials, who insisted on kissing each person who fell into their grasp. Before boarding the bus, some of the women stared plaintively back toward the 727. These were the ones with loved ones still aboard.

A dim glow in the east marked where the full moon was rising through the overcast.

Never once did McCoy's eyes click toward the darkness on the starboard side of the aircraft. He felt certain he was being watched—and wanted none of the three

Shi'ites now aboard tipped off that Peterson and his "Arab commandos" were crawling through the short but dense scrub bordering the apron.

Colonel Alexander's voice intruded on his concentration. "Section One, acknowledge that you're still on hold."

McCoy frowned, knowing full well that Woodbridge in Washington had compelled Alexander to ask this. "All sections are in place and still on hold. Waiting for last female now. Can see her standing in front entry now, talking to someone unseen. Can you make him from your angle, Bobby?"

"Uh, negative, Section One," he said from his ambulance, which was parked forward of the aircraft. "Whoever this boy is, he's snuggled up against the cockpit door. We got some wary folks aboard that bird."

"That's it," McCoy whispered, his voice higher by half a pitch as he watched the last stewardess whisk down the chute. "She's out, Nick. And the back stairs are still down. Advise."

"Stand by, all sections."

"No, no, no," McCoy groaned to himself as Alexander checked one more time with Washington. He clenched the steering wheel as the rattling engines of the Mercedes sedan and the shuttle bus were fired up and the vehicles crept back toward the terminal. "They're going to screw it up again . . . they're going to screw it up again."

But then he could tell from Alexander's first breathless syllable.

"All Delta sections—you've got a go. Take 'em down."

McCoy purged his lungs of the air he'd been hoarding, then drove across the tarmac until the fuel truck was positioned forward of the port wing. He set the parking brake and made sure the cuff of the maintenance jump suit had not snagged on the leg-holstered .45 automatic caliber pistol he had strapped to his calf. The operator sitting beside him picked his Ingram MAC-10 submachine gun up off the floorboard and held it at the ready against the door.

Bobby Lee and then Doctor Jack inched their ambulances to within thirty feet of the nose wheel.

For the first time—and furtively—McCoy made sure none of Peterson's people were visible while creeping through the scrub. The ragged profile of brush was unbroken by human forms.

The passenger window shades were down, but as of this instant no one had thought to close the front entry door or retract the airstairs. Of the nine hatches on a 727, two were wide open—unbelievable luck.

"All right—show time," McCoy told the operator beside him, then got out and removed the ladder from the rear of the truck. Keeping the boom mike side of his face turned away from the plane, he approached the leading edge of the wing, set the ladder up and went back for the hose, reeling it off at what he hoped appeared to be a leisurely work pace.

The refueling connectors were under the wing on a 727, but that didn't concern McCoy as he clambered on top. The flight for Beirut had burned up half of the plane's range, and the last thing he wanted to do was to give the hijackers a full eight thousand gallons of JP-5 to play with —enough to fly all the way to Iran.

He stuck the four-inch hose into a probe that didn't exist and pretended to fill the number-one wing integral fuel tank. He had an operational reason for being on the wing—and put it into effect by rocking back and forth on his feet as heavily as he could.

A window shade shot up, then was quickly pulled down again. His little dance had been telegraphed to the tourist cabin.

"That's right, boys," McCoy whispered, "it's just the grease monkey, who's going to lube you in about one minute."

Practice with a Boeing 727 made available to Delta by the FAA had revealed that when the entry teams climbed on the wings, the motion could be detected inside the aircraft.

McCoy smiled to himself. Now the terrs would dismiss that movement as just the maintenance crew poking around.

Arms akimbo, he faced away from the fuselage and keyed his mike. "Okay, Delta, let's do it. Close communications. We go in sixty seconds. Radios off the air."

Besides not wanting his operations sergeants distracted by chatter filling their heads during these critical moments, McCoy also knew all too well that in fifty-two seconds no one was going to hear anything but the most god-awful series of bangs ever experienced at close range. These would be accompanied by the kind of flashes that would make a terrorist think he had been given a ringside seat at the Creation.

Finally it was a go—he could hardly believe it.

Thirty seconds.

Using the inside of his forearm, McCoy felt under the maintenance uniform for the ultra-high-speed drill attached to his body harness. This he would use to implant the explosive charge that would shuck off the overwing escape hatch on his side. And Peterson's team, after mounting the starboard wing with a padded, lightweight, collapsible ladder, would deal with the opposite hatch in the same way.

Two operatives had been given an expressway by the hijackers' stupidity in leaving down the airstairs. Never had the team ever anticipated being given such an entry windfall.

As long as the front door remained wide open, Bobby's section would, after tossing in silent ignition stun grenades, hurl its smallest member up and through the opening.

Like ski jumping, the first time was the worst, this

human cannonball of a trooper claimed, having made the practice flight a hundred times.

Twenty to go.

Bobby would then streak up a ladder hung from the lip of the front door by his entry man. He would aim his bullhorn and unmistakably American accent into the cabins. "Down! Keep your heads down! Get down on the floor!"

Then Delta would earn its pay.

Ten.

McCoy's hand began unzipping the top of his coveralls.

15

2232 Hours

As soon as Nick Alexander saw the brunette stewardess getting out of the white Mercedes, he knew she was the one to talk to.

He had just come down the elevator, trying to raise McCoy on the sly with the transceiver—without Colonel Aziz seeing. But it was no good. There was no response from Section One. And Aziz proudly explained that the cage was made from the finest Japanese steel. "It is the most modern elevator in Algeria." Then, for the third time since Alexander had crashed through the room full of VIPs, who were then polishing off a course of falafel and Coca-Cola, Aziz begged, "Please, it is more appropriate that you observe from the balcony. Appreciate the extraordinary delicacy with which my government must pursue this affair."

"I've got to talk to some of those hostages."

"I will bring a few to the balcony."

"No time," Alexander snapped, forcing back the elevator doors as soon as they cracked open and then half trotting down a long corridor to the front of the terminal.

As far as the condition of the first hostages to be helped out of the shuttle bus, he'd seen VC stumble out of caves with both ears bleeding after a B-52 pounding who were more composed than some of these people. He didn't blame them for their condition. As much as anyone who had not personally experienced the ego-shattering horrors of being a hostage, he knew what these women and children had suffered in the eternity since this morning.

But he needed someone with her shit in one bag—and fast too.

The brunette stewardess refused the offer of a hand as she stepped out of the Mercedes, thinking to adjust the hem of her skirt as she swung her legs around. Although clearly exhausted, her face bruised, she seemed aware, even appreciative of her surroundings. Alexander had honed a special critical perception in order to select his own personnel for Delta, and he now saw in this young woman the same thing he looked for in potential operators. She had already dug deep within herself, more than any reasonable human being could ask of herself, yet she would dig deeper if she could be convinced of the need.

With Aziz still jabbering behind him, Alexander approached her. "Excuse me."

For a moment she was startled by the dark cammies. "Who are—?"

"Colonel Alexander, United States Army."

"Oh." She wiped a strand of hair out of her eyes. "I'm Gretti Werner."

"The purser."

"Yes, Colonel, the purser."

"Listen, I don't have much time—and I urgently need some information."

She blinked at him a moment, then turned her face toward the distant aircraft. "What is going to happen? Is something going to happen?"

No use lying to this one. "Yes, soldiers are going to enter the plane to rescue the remaining hostages."

"Yes," Aziz butted in, "our elite commandos. Everything will be well. Everything will be peaceful."

"No!" Gretti cried. "You must stop them!"

Checking the 727, Alexander thought he could see a tiny figure on the wing—McCoy, undoubtedly, seconds away from effecting his entry into the cabin. "Why? Tell me why?"

"They will kill the other hostages in Beirut. They took the Marines and the Jews off the plane when the other hijackers came on board!"

Alexander felt his commanding view of the Maze collapse to ground level again. *What other hijackers?*

"Those who rushed out of the food truck. Twelve of them with rifles. All of them had big rifles."

Alexander broke out his transceiver—secrecy be damned. "All sections! Code Red! It's off! Acknowledge!"

He boosted the volume, but only static hissed back at him.

"Code Red, Delta! Acknowledge, goddammit!"

"This is Zap Three."

"Go, Winnemucca."

"The entry sections shut down communications about thirty ago. They're moving in."

"Give them a red-star cluster—fast."

"Affirm."

Alexander was already dragging the MP out from behind the jeep's wheel when the 40mm flare projectile burst into a disappointingly dim festoon—the overcast was muting much of its effect.

Then he had to fend off Aziz by straight-arming him.

"Colonel Alexander! Such obvious intervention is not

permitted by the agreement between our governments! You yourself were party to this understanding—"

"I know." Jamming the stick into reverse, Alexander scattered a covey of paramilitary types, who didn't know whether to shoot or salute as his brake lamps came closer and closer.

Then he roared off between the shuttle bus and the Mercedes, hitting the toggle switches for the blue flasher mounted on the rollbar and the foreign-sounding high-low siren. Afraid this was not enough, he began flicking the headbeams on and off. "Goddammit! Shut it down, Scottie!"

Skidding in a four-wheel drift away from the tarmac and putting the cockpit lights of the 727 dead ahead, he took a hard bounce across a shallow ditch that cost him his wind when his chest struck the wheel.

But he continued across the darkened scrub toward the plane.

Scott McCoy couldn't believe it. First a star cluster popping off and now some kind of emergency rig brush-busting this way from the terminal. Was Alexander out of his mind to let the Algerians commit this lunacy in the hair-trigger seconds before the most difficult entry of all: one into a crowded aircraft cabin?

Then it occurred to him with a sinking feeling that Delta had been double-crossed—and Alexander was himself a hostage at this moment.

Still, they had to go. There was no stopping now. The high-speed drill was poised in his hands, ready to zip through the skin of the fuselage in the vicinity of the hinges of the hatch.

"Mustafa! Brothers!" a voice screamed from the front door. "The Americans!"

This was followed by a burst of distinctive-sounding Kalashnikov fire from the airstairs—which could then be heard being cranked up.

The rounds had not whistled anywhere near McCoy,

but he saw that the tank on the fuel truck was issuing two streams of kerosene onto the tarmac. He waved for the operator who had just stepped out of the cab in order to cover him with a MAC-10 to get back inside. "Drive it away!"

Behind him the engines vibrated to life and began sucking air past him.

Another burst of automatic rifle fire flashed in the corner of his eye—this time from the front door. He went flat against the fuselage. "Shit!"

Bobby and his section had piled out of the ambulances and were halfway to the plane when McCoy shouted over the now-deafening thunder of turbofans, "Get back! Don't shoot!"

He could see Doctor Jack looking under the aircraft as he withdrew, giving Peterson's section the abort signal.

A Kalashnikov barked again, and McCoy went prone on the wing, thinking of the fuel tank directly beneath him. But when the long burst expended one magazine, and the hijacker could be heard slapping in a second clip, McCoy realized that the fire was not directed against him but at the inflatable escape chute. The hijacker finished cutting it in two with a quick stutter of rounds, but didn't close the door as soon as the slide had fallen away.

Rolling off the outboard side of the wing, McCoy hit the tarmac on all fours and kept scrambling toward the darkness.

Suddenly the anticollision light atop the 727 winked on, giving an eerie stroboscopic effect to the scene. Between the instantaneous intervals of blackness, McCoy could glimpse Bobby's section jerkily sprinting for cover behind the ambulances.

The operator who had backed away the fuel truck was now leaning over its hood, peering down the stubby length of his MAC-10 at the front door of the aircraft. Fuel was staining the tarmac around its ruptured tank in an ever-widening circle.

"Get away from that truck!" McCoy cried.

The man ran a few meters, then dived headlong into the scrub.

McCoy heard no reports from the plane, but he realized, faintly, almost abstractly, that he had been picked up and thrown a distance, that his clothes and his hair had been singed—and that the truck was a huge, orange fireball.

"McCoy!" Alexander was squatting behind a jeep with a blue light still rotating on its rollbar. "Are you all right?"

He took a step, and didn't sink into an invisible quagmire, as he had immediately after being hit in the leg during Tet. "Yes," he said, crouching beside Alexander. "What the fuck happened?"

"Code Red . . . it's off!"

Rounds dinged against the opposite side of the jeep and took out the windshield.

"But we had them! We could have taken them!"

Alexander shook his head no.

Flight 827 had begun to taxi.

"Americans!" Foolishly insane, one of the hijackers was filling the door from side to side.

"Merry Christmas." McCoy reached for his .45. The Shi'ite's face wasn't more than fifty feet away. "This is almost too easy."

But he had no sooner drawn on the careless figure than Alexander forced down his arm. "There are twelve more terrs on board than we thought!"

"What!"

"They took on reinforcements in Beirut!"

McCoy's eyes had not strayed from the front entry door, and now he stiffened as a young man was jostled to the yawning edge, made to stand with bound hands in front of the hijacker, who now took what looked like a Beretta from his belt and jabbed it against the back of the hostage's head.

"That's a military haircut, Nick!" McCoy almost wailed. "He's one of us! That guy is one of our own!"

"Delta—hold all fire!" Alexander shouted. Then he called out to the hijacker: "Talk to us!"

"Now maybe your cowboy President will believe that we are serious!" The hijacker forced the Marine to bend over. Then he shot him in the base of the skull.

The body tumbled out onto the apron, and the door swung shut.

The shadow of the fuselage rippled over the crumpled shape, mercifully removing it from McCoy's sight. But then the plane was wheeling starboard onto the runaway, and the dead Marine was lit by the waning flames of the fuel truck once again.

The pilot went to full throttle.

Looking dismayed, Peterson trotted over to McCoy and Alexander, ripping off the *khaffiyeh* and using it to wipe the sweat and paint off his face. "Zap Two says he's got a clear shot at the nose-wheel tire. He wants instructions."

"Tell him negative," Alexander said.

The plane lifted off. Within seconds it was gone.

Silently, Delta converged on the body. Someone lit it with a flashlight.

Taking out his knife, Bobby Lee jerk-cut the bindings that had slowly turned the hands the ugly purple of a bruise.

Alexander's eyes were watery. They caught the brightness of the risen moon. Everyone except McCoy was careful not to look at him.

"In case anybody's wondering," the colonel finally said, "why we couldn't save this man, the Shi'ites got reinforced during their stopover in Beirut. There were twelve more automatic weapons in that 727 than we planned on. Had we not pulled back, sixty Americans, not one, would be dead right now." He paused. When he spoke again, he sounded more in control of his voice. "Okay, somebody break out a poncho. Get him covered up. I'll be goddamned if some motherfucker is going to make money off a photo of a kid who went the distance for his country."

McCoy walked away from the others. He looked eastward. The moon was shining brightly through a rent in the cloud cover.

After a minute or two, someone strolled up behind him. He knew without looking that it was Alexander.

"Where do we go now, Nick?"

Alexander lit up a Winston. "After them." Before he could shake out the match, a sob escaped him, leaving him with a startled expression that was caught by the brief glow. Then he threw down the cigarette. "We go after the sons of bitches, Scottie."

#

18 June 1985 . . . 1500 Hours

He sat in the very back of the tourist-class cabin because he always sat as close to the tail assembly as possible when flying. This increased his chances of survival, and Raffi Amir was an authority on survival, although he was also a self-avowed fatalist. It was a funny combination; nevertheless, it worked for him. And didn't he have a little salt mixed in with the pepper of his curly head of hair to prove it?

This achievement of reaching forty-nine years had not come easily. By trial and error, he had learned all about risk-taking. Good risks. Bad risks. Tragic risks like in Shakespeare or something. And fun risks. Like today's, maybe.

He wore a sports coat but no tie. Sighing out loud, he reached in his bulging pocket and brought out a ripe pomegranate. A gift from a friend on a kibbutz who probably kept the best ones for himself.

Noticing the stains already marring his white shirt and trousers, Raffi took his handkerchief out of his front trouser pocket and spread it over his lap. Then, silently asking his wife to thank him for this consideration to her laundry tasks, he broke apart the thick husk of the fruit with his long fingers.

He offered some seeds to the figure beside him, but the fellow kept hogging the window seat in stony silence. "Well," Raffi muttered, "perhaps you have your own worries, yes?"

A tram hauling a string of baggage containers putted around a hangar and pulled alongside the Boeing 727-200F. "What, more baggage?" He reached into his inner coat pocket and took out a small, clear plastic case containing two pairs of earplugs. "Take, take," he offered— but once again was ignored, so he shrugged and quickly stopped up his own ear canals. "You'll be sorry."

Snugging the pomegranate firmly between his thick legs, Raffi then covered his face with his palms.

In lightning succession, there were three muffled explosions, each from a different place around the plane. But these were firecrackers compared to what came next: a light so godly it shone right through Raffi's hands, coloring his vision orange as the stuff propagated right through his flesh. The hopelessly disorienting blasts followed, five, one right after the other. The drumbeats of Armageddon.

He made sure he sat perfectly still, for when he could see again there were dark shapes at the far end of the cabin, and suddenly at its center too, shooting pistols. Shooting pistols very well—because the fellow next to

Raffi shuddered twice, then slumped forward.

"*Ein breira,*" he consoled the fellow. *There is no choice.*

"Clear!" the American operator shouted, slipping his .45 back into the holster on his body harness, walking purposely back to Raffi. "Well?" he asked, reaching across him to force the cloth dummy upright in the window seat again.

Where the bridge of the nose should have been were two squashed wax bullets.

"Very nice. And thank you for blowing the hatches off. Tourist class needed a bit of a breeze." Smiling, Raffi turned as Colonel Alexander came through the port rear door, clutching a stopwatch. *Great posture. If I had posture like that, I wouldn't have a belly like this.* Unconsciously, Raffi began rubbing his stomach, which was hiding his belt.

"Twenty seconds," Alexander said. "Major Scott McCoy, may I introduce Raffi Amir of Mossad."

The major hiked an eyebrow. He seemed a bit surprised. "*Israeli* intelligence?"

"Indeed." Raffi unbuckled his belt, then suddenly laughed. "Look what your flash-bang grenade made me do!" The pomegranate had been crushed between his legs. He began dabbing at the red stain with a corner of the handkerchief he had moistened with his tongue.

"Pleased to meet you," the major said. "It gave me a bit of a surprise."

"To see a live dummy out here?"

Simpering, McCoy nodded.

"Yes, well, ours is the business of taking surprises in stride. Is it not?" Rising, Raffi frowned one last time at the indelible stain on his trousers. Then, assuring himself that his Smith & Wesson .357 Magnum was still snugly in its shoulder holster, he gestured for Alexander to lead the way outside.

From the ground he shook his head at the twisted and

blackened remnants of the port-side engine. "This, gentlemen, was an El Al cargo plane—before it ran afoul of a Palestinian rocket. Luckily, its pilot was landing at the time. Otherwise . . ." He purposely did not finish. "So, when we heard your Delta Force was coming to Israel, we put some seats in. Nice job, what?"

"We appreciate your anticipating our needs, Mr. Amir," Alexander said.

"Call me Raffi, please." Sadly, he shook his head at the engine again. "A good phrase."

"Sir?"

"*Anticipating our needs.* Israel is too small, beset by two many enemies, to ever do anything but that." He suddenly brightened. "Colonel Alexander, both you gentlemen, I would consider it an honor if you would share an early dinner with my family and me. We can discuss matters along the way. I promise not to keep you long. Later this evening I must fly up north to Safad."

"Thank you," Alexander began, "but I don't know if I'd feel right about leaving my people—"

"I'll stay, Colonel," McCoy said. "I'll get this drill down to ten seconds, then let them knock off for some well-deserved R and R."

"See, Colonel, it's settled. And I can have you back here by helicopter in five minutes."

Alexander gestured at his dusty Gore-Tex jump suit. "I don't know if I'm dressed for—"

"Colonel Alexander, for Israel that is white tie and tails. Okay? Okay."

Nick Alexander squeezed his big frame into the front seat of the battered, vintage Fiat.

"Excuse the mess," Raffi said. "This is also my family car. My wife is a cellist."

The back was cluttered with loose sheet music, shopping sacks filled with pomegranates, and a soccer ball. Protruding out from under Raffi's broken-down seat was the barrel of an Uzi SMG. *So this is life on the front lines of world terrorism,* Alexander thought to himself. He could easily imagine Raffi stopping off on his way home at the local convenience market to pick up a bottle of California vin rosé, a ripe avocado and a box of 9mm parabellum ammunition.

"Is this your first time in Israel, Colonel?"

"Nick. If you're Raffi, I'm Nick."

"Sure." The intelligence officer laughed softly, ignoring the indifferent salute from the sentry manning the well-fortified main gate to the air base, turning onto a busy boulevard that could have been in Dallas or Los Angeles at the same hour—except that, within two miles, Alexander counted three light armored vehicles and two troop trucks.

"No, I was here once before in the sixties. A stopover of two days before I went on to the Shah's Iran. But I didn't get around much."

Raffi was silent for few minutes, then said, "My trip tonight involves your hostages."

Alexander sat straighter. "Have your operatives located them?"

"Well, let us say that they have eliminated some distressing possibilities."

"Such as?"

"The hostages are not in a Druze village in the Shouf Mountains—or worse yet, under the control of Hizbollah in the Bekaa Valley."

"Are your people sure they've been taken off the plane?"

"Yes—all but the captain and his crew."

"Level with me, Raffi—where do you think they are?"

"West Beirut somewhere. But please don't go telling your President that before I have this meeting tonight in Safad. Under these circumstances, with no one saying anything on either side of the Green Line in Beirut, we must rely on people who ordinarily would not warrant our trust."

Alexander caught Raffi's eye. "We want those bastards—bad."

"Israel *wants* you to have those bastards, Nick. You must believe that—and trust that we will give you every scrap of reliable information we discover. But facts are not easy to bring out of as confused a country as poor Lebanon." He veered up a dirt driveway to a modest cinder-block house. There were sapling olive and orange trees out front, and a tiny patch of lawn that was not doing well. Raffi had to toot the horn twice before a small boy darted from a side yard to move his bicycle out of the carport.

Alexander thought he had masked his surprise when introduced to Mrs. Amir, a handsome woman in her mid-twenties who was rocking a sleeping baby girl in her arms. Yet, while his host retired to the kitchen to mix drinks, she said gracefully, as if she had read the question in Alexander's eyes and found it perfectly natural: "We are Raffi's second family. His first wife and son were killed by a bomb. It happened on a bus not a kilometer from here."

Suddenly, grinning, Raffi burst from the kitchen, holding a flesh-toned earplug in each hand instead of a glass. "Look what I forgot to take out! You, Nick, I thought you were just soft-spoken. But you"—his eyes laughed warmly at his wife—"well, you know what I thought . . ."

17

Georges had the best car in all of Beirut.

The hand-buffed black Mercedes was far more dignified than the nondescript vehicles the American Ambassador had been compelled to use instead of his Cadillac limousine. Georges's Mercedes was already such a symbol of Shi'ite determination no one thought to adorn it with portraits of the Ayatollah Khomeini or the missing Imam Musa al Sadr, as all the other cars and trucks in the long line had been.

The convoy had been assembled under the protection of the Amal militia on the grounds of the Hippodrome Racetrack, a symbol of French colonial decadence that had been shelled to rubble during the fighting between the Israelis and the Palestinians.

Abdul relaxed on the comfortable back seat of the Mercedes, sipping tea through a sugar cube he clenched between his front teeth. Georges was still outside, arguing with several of his lieutenants at once.

Amal, Abdul smirked. He had been unable to convince the militiamen that the commandos he had seen at the Algiers airport were Americans, not Algerians.

Georges was now screaming and wildly gesticulating at his officers. He had not wanted to assemble the hostages at the Hippodrome in the first place; he felt that it was too close to Rue de Damas, better known as the Green Line. This was the no-man's-land between the Moslem and Christian halves of the city that was periodically overgrown with brush, especially whenever the strife continued without pause for several months.

Abdul had not liked the idea of all the hostages being gathered in one place inside West Beirut. He had said so

97

at this morning's conference. What he really wanted was to have the Americans shuttled in small groups to the Abdullah Military Barracks near Baalbek in eastern Lebanon. But Amal was not prepared to surrender control of the captives.

Immediately after their arrival at Beirut Airport from the American fiasco at Algiers, all the hostages—except the ATW crew, who remained aboard the plane under Jaffar's protection—had been divvied up into "disciplinary cells" of five or six men each and dispersed throughout Ras Beirut, a virtual compound of Islamic militias.

But then an unmanageable *bey* had decided that he could do better by opening talks directly with the Gemayel government over the release of the half dozen hostages in his hands. Within an hour Amal relieved him of his burden—at gunpoint. And Georges had to admit, in a hemming and hawing way, that he personally did not have the degree of authority necessary to keep tabs on the hostages as long as they were held in so many different locations and under the thumbs of so many subgroups. He then instructed all factions to bring their hostages blindfolded to the Municipal Stadium. But then it had been learned that one of the Druze militias had mined the playing field during the night, so Georges's lieutenants had recommended making the Hippodrome the rendezvous point.

Abdul had argued that the Americans had satellites that could see a man on the ground picking his nose. But, smiling, Georges said that religious parades were as common as automatic rifles in Beirut.

So Abdul had given up and decided to just go along for the ride. He was still tired from the hijacking—but tired in a good and mellow way. Mustafa, Jaffar and he had become celebrities, although they were lionized in a quiet way so as not to betray them to Phalangist spies, of whom there were many even in West Beirut.

Georges hurried back to the Mercedes, pursued by a

furious lieutenant, whom he ignored as he got inside. "Quickly," he said to his driver, "pull away."

"What route?"

"Ah . . . down Boulevard Saeb Salaam." Then, shaking his head, he said to Abdul, "This is unbelievable—at the last minute they don't want the hostages so near the beach."

"Perhaps they are right."

"No, no . . ." Georges jerked a starched French cuff out of his coat sleeve. "Our biggest concern at this point is a raid by the Christian militias across the Green Line."

"What about an Israeli attack by sea?"

"Israel will not involve itself in this. It is America's problem." One of two bodyguards in the front seat poured him a cup of tea from a thermos. "And America learned a bitter lesson from that Iran rescue foolishness. A disaster. Even they admitted so."

Abdul glanced through the rear window. The line of vehicles had fallen in behind the Mercedes. The black-hooded hostages could not be seen. They were jammed down on the floorboards of the sedans or concealed in the beds of covered trucks. The fenders, roofs and hoods of all the cars were crowded with rifle-toting militiamen.

"You must tell me something, Georges."

"Yes, my brother."

"I read this in the newspaper. When Mustafa and I first landed at the airport here, you told the press that Amal would not talk to criminals who would commit such a terrible act."

Georges met Abdul's stare, then looked out at the window. He waved at some old men sitting before a cafe, puffing on the surgical tubing they had attached to their elaborate, silver-plated hookahs. "It meant nothing, my brother. Politics. We required a certain credibility before we could negotiate for the release of our people being held in Israel."

A gang of cheering youths with white headbands

approached the Mercedes, firing their Kalashnikovs into the air. Several of the hot casings skittered across the polished hood of Georges's car before coming to rest along a crack, and he shouted to one of the bodyguards, "Out! Get them off! They will ruin the finish!"

The man leaped out and swatted the brass hulls away, warning the youths to stand aside or take a few rounds from his M-3 grease gun. Then as he tried to return to the front seat again, Georges told him and his partner, "Ride on the fenders to prevent more of this hooliganism. Both of you."

"But I cannot see when they ride on the fenders," the driver said.

"All of you—do as I say!" Then Georges calmed himself with a sip of tea. "Look at this." He pointed at mounds of uncollected garbage on the sidewalks. "Terrible. Didn't we send a detail to clean this street up yesterday?"

No one said anything.

From a broken main a torrent of water was rushing down the gutter. Here and there corpulent, half-wild cats were poised on the curb, waiting for pieces of edible flotsam to whisk down to them. Abdul was reminded of a Walt Disney film he had enjoyed as a boy. Big bears waiting for salmon to flash up out of white waters. His faint smile ran off his lips. Once he had taken his daughter to that *cine* near Place des Martyrs. Another Disney film: *Davy Crockett.* The cannons had scared her.

The driver was laying on the horn.

"Whose roadblock is this?" Georges asked. "There were to be no roadblocks on Avenue du General de Gaulle this morning!"

The bodyguards bounced off the fenders and moved warily up to a dozen men in rumpled, dusty uniforms. Two of the unidentified soldiers, Abdul realized as he reached for his Beretta and held it against his thigh, were armed with LAWs, antitank rockets—disposable like everything else the Americans offered, including their friendship.

The troops looked like Shi'ites, but who could be certain?

One of the bodyguards jogged back to Georges's side of the Mercedes.

Georges rolled down the bullet-resistant glass of his window, but only a few inches. "Who are they?"

"Until last night they were with Lebanese Forces. But they deserted. Now they call themselves . . ." The guard lapsed into an embarrassed silence. "I forget what they call themselves—but they are brothers. I think I know one of them."

"What are they doing erecting a roadblock here?"

"Collecting contributions for . . . for whatever they now call themselves."

"This manner of extortion must cease," Georges said, taking a thick sheaf of Lebanese pound notes out of his wallet. "Here—and hurry."

"They insist on American dollars."

Sighing, Abdul handed the man a hundred-dollar bill. He avoided Abdul's glare. "It is not an afternoon to quibble."

The soldiers dragged a wooden barrier of concertina wire out of the street, and the convey crept forward. Georges's militiamen emptied their rifles into the sky as a gesture of solidarity with the newly formed Moslem faction.

Abdul found himself longing for the singularity of purpose one felt in the Bekaa community. There, it was a holy war, not this unholy squabble that never accomplished anything.

"Take this side street here," Georges said to the driver. "Someone told me a building collapsed across Rue el Assad last night."

The rocky point of land, the westernmost projection of the city into the Mediterranean, was shared by a former

French garrison and a Maronite Catholic church and school complex. The garrison had been converted into an Amal brigade headquarters. With its concrete bunker facing the sea and a bomb shelter basement, it was the stoutest stronghold of any militia unit in Beirut. It was where the two surviving Marine hostages had been immediately taken from the airport.

They were waved through a lightly manned sentry station and continued up a narrow lane, past an antiaircraft gun emplacement in a small vineyard near the shore.

"Until now," Georges said as the Mercedes sped down the narrow lane that separated the two facilities, "we have left the Maronite place alone."

"How many Christians are still there?"

"Only one. An elderly monk. The priest and the rest of the parish fled to the east side. They left Brother John behind to watch the property. There he is now."

The Mercedes parked beside a white Volkswagen van with *Mount Lebanon Maronite School* painted on its side. A gray-bearded man stood nearby, snipping at a rosebush with a pair of rusted clippers. He looked up in surprise at the boisterous convoy, then recognized Georges through the window and smiled at him.

"Is he simple?" Abdul tapped his forehead with a finger.

"Exceedingly. But very useful at times. Anytime Amnesty International or the United Nations comes calling on us, I take them over to meet Brother John al-Khazen. How can Amal be intolerant if we count Maronite monks among our dear friends?"

Abdul glowered at the old man in a worn cloak with long, flowing sleeves. "It is difficult to believe that we share some of the same blood."

"Come, I will introduce you."

Strolling away from the Mercedes, Abdul returned the congratulatory waves of militiamen hanging out the windows of the old garrison.

"Brother John, I would like to introduce you to Abdullah, a very good friend of mine."

The old man nodded feebly.

Abdul turned away from him.

"Brother," Georges went on, "we will have need of your grounds for a short time—if you have no objection."

"I have no objection." He had the thin voice of a very old man. "And it is always good to see you, Monsieur Georges."

"Excellent. Now if you will pardon us . . ."

The monk bowed and shuffled off toward his bullet-pocked church.

The Amal leader then motioned for one of his lieutenants to approach him. Mustafa tagged along with the officer, grinning boyishly from the excitement of so much activity.

"Selim, see to it that some mattresses are thrown down in the gymnasium."

"How many, Georges?"

"Fifty. Oh, yes—and six more for the basement cells."

The lieutenant's eyes widened. "Where will I find so many?"

"Search inside the ruined hotels. Now, Mustafa—"

"Sir?"

"I would consider it a personal favor if you would take charge of the Americans we keep here at the school. This will exhibit a certain continuity . . . a completeness of action."

"And if any rescue is attempted," Abdul added, "all of the hostages must die."

"It will be done, my brothers." He ran back to the convoy to hurry the off-loading of the Americans from the vehicles.

"Now . . ." Georges put his arm around Abdul's shoulders—but only briefly. "You will be given command of the eight special prisoners, who will be kept apart from the others.

"The Jews?"

Georges nodded as if thinking of something else. "Keep them separate from the Marines." Avoiding the thorns, he snapped a rose off its stem and sniffed it. "Ah, delicious. You should have seen these gardens ten years ago."

"I did," Abdul snapped. "I also had a home and a family in this city ten years ago."

"Oh, I meant nothing by what I said." George tried to reassure him with a pat on the arm, but once again Abdul bristled at his touch. "And I promise you, my brother, whatever happens during the talks, the Zionists will be the last to be released . . . if they are released at all."

They were clear, sweet-sounding bells that could be heard two or three miles inside the city when the evening breeze was onshore like this. Brother John rang out the same sequence of notes twice, then let go of the rope.

The exertion had left him a bit winded.

He checked his wristwatch: 6:45. Thirty minutes to wait. But he would use those minutes well.

Picking up his oversized copy of the *Kitab al-Huda,* the *Book of Guidance,* off the belfry stairs, he hobbled outside on a weak ankle that had just been worsened by his riding the bell ropes. Pausing under the expansive Aleppo pine, he shaded his eyes against the flat rays of the sunset. The sea was a deep rose color. Lovely.

Picking up his feet now, he followed the path down to the promontory and the marble bench on which he meditated at this time each evening, except during the sudden storms that drenched his precious retreat.

Across the small cove, on their own point of stony land, the Amal militiamen waved at him, then went back to planting another iron pipe in the hard ground with the aid of a gasoline-powered posthole digger. In the past few hours, they had erected at least a dozen of these poles, until every open place near the headquarters or school was a forest of them. He wondered what use they might serve? Were they antennae of some sort?

The monk opened the flaking leather-bound tome. Inside was a stubby little pencil and a piece of graph paper, the kind he had passed out years before to his geometry students. He wondered how many of them had died since those more peaceful days, but then shrugged off the painful speculation.

Carefully, almost controlling his palsied grasp, he sketched in the sewer pipe jutting out into the shallows; the old bunker, its concrete facing scaling off; the precise dimensions of the garrison, the church and the big brick school building.

Long ago, so along ago he now smiled in recollection of the person he had once been, he had eaten, slept and learned the arts of war in that shabby-looking headquarters. He had served in the Forces Franaise Liban, the colonial occupation army.

Now, humming a liturgical song to himself, he sketched in an imaginary artillery barrage over the shining beach, the dug-in antiaircraft gun, the courtyard crowded with armored vehicles, and onto the barracks itself, which flew apart into fire and smoke.

Self-critically, he compared his final sketch to the familiar scene before his eyes. One could not be too meticulous when it came to intelligence. He had spent the entire day finding out as much as he could without arousing Amal's suspicion.

Closing the book on his handiwork, he rose and, on an impulse, took the path that led up the slope to the school building. The militiaman at the door politely refused to let him pass, so he walked along the west wall of the gymnasium.

At a wire-glass window, a young man was staring out

across the now iron-colored waves, his sensitive-looking features very unhappy.

A young American, the monk reminded himself, smiling and blessing the young man with the cross.

He smiled back at Brother John, mouthing some words the monk could not read.

Brother John checked his watch again, then limped on toward the church.

For hundreds of years, his people, the Maronites, had remained a Catholic island, loyal to the Holy See in Rome, but cast adrift in an Islamic sea. For this reason they had always relied on alliances with outsiders: first the Crusaders, later the French, then the Israelis, and most recently the Americans, whose young Marines had perished so miserably, so unexpectedly for Lebanon's sake.

Brother John entered the darkened vestibule through the main doors which, as in all Maronite churches, faced westward. He continued down the aisle, his footfalls echoing loudly, reminding him of the emptiness that now oppressed this place. Passing through the chancel, hauntingly silent of choir voices, he then shuffled behind the altar, stooped with a creaking of his knees, and felt along the base for the concealed latch. A panel popped open—the door to a compartment from which he removed the battered M1 field radio given to him by a former student, now a colonel in the Phalangist militia.

Seven-fifteen—it was time.

The code he had pealed out on the church bells was used to alert Phalangist headquarters in East Beirut that he had a message to send in thirty minutes. Transmission time was kept as brief as possible. This was so that Soviet-trained communications technicians in the Moslem forces would have a more difficult time locating the source of these mysterious dialogues in Syriac, a dead language derived from Aramaic—the tongue spoken by Christ, the brother had often reminded his pupils.

At least one of them had learned it well. And he now

esponded from the Christian side of the city.

Brother John tilted his sketch toward the light from a stained-glass window.

18

2100 Hours . . . Israel

Bobby Lee had found a guitar someone had abandoned on the small bandstand. After ten minutes, he gave up trying to tune it and, despite protests from the other operators, began strumming something or other he thought he remembered.

"What's the name of that anyways?" Doctor Jack hollered, looking up from his medical bag.

"Fuck you all."

The medic nodded. "I thought I recognized it."

The Quonset was the Israeli equivalent of an EM club, although tonight all their personnel, enlisted or otherwise, had been barred and the place given over to Delta.

There were a dozen or so fifties-style malt shop booths, red Naugahyde repaired where needed with orange vinyl tape. Bobby sat alone at one, the guitar laid flat on the table. Pausing to take a swig of beer, he frowned at McCoy, who was poring over the same plasticized map of Beirut he had been studying since chow. Peterson was sprawled across three folding chairs he'd pulled together, his arm thrown across his eyes to block out the humming neon lights.

For the third time in an hour, some Israelis pounded at the front door. When no one answered, the others had strolled away; but an operator reported from the venetian blinds that this group was lingering under the floodlamp, as if they didn't know where to go next. "Hey, wait—these troops are amazons."

"Repeat?"

"*Womens*, Bobby Lee," the operator said with precise diction. "Womens shouldering M-16s."

"Ah, you just added that to make me horny."

"Heh, boss," Winnemucca asked McCoy, "what do you say we let them in?"

"Sounds like an old Indian trick to me," another operator warned. "Remember what he done to them little *Hausfraus* out for an evening in Wiesbaden?"

"They had it coming," Waukene said with a slight smile.

"Oh, shit, Winnemucca—they probably had it coming a dozen ways that night, and not one they'd ever seen done before."

"Our ladies are departing, gentlemen," the scout reported from the blinds. "We are losing our insertion opportunity."

Everyone was now looking to McCoy, who, pensively, took a long draught of beer, then set down his mug. He smiled—it seemed like the first time since before Algiers. "Now listen up. Alexander will have my ass for this"—the smile blossomed into a grin—"but we are helicopter mechanics here to service the junk we sold them. So go ahead and catch those amazons, somebody, before they get away."

A cheer went up, and Winnemucca slid the two-by-four bar out of its brackets behind the door. Several operators were giving one another hand jive, and Doctor Jack was pounding the table, demanding to know where he could get some champagne—fast.

Yet when Winnemucca led a file of ten young women inside, the clamor in the Quonset died away.

An awkward silence followed until McCoy said, "I am Sergeant Al York—and these are the men of the Sixty-ninth Helicopter Squadron."

"Americans?" the one in the baggiest fatigues of all asked.

"Yes."

"Oh!" she exhaled, lightly touching Waukene's forearm in apology. "We were afraid you might be Egyptians!"

Bobby Lee laughed until there were tears in his eyes, then joined the others in throwing pieces of half-eaten sandwiches at the Paiute operator, who answered their effronteries with war whoops.

A few moments later a young women sat down across from Bobby. "Do you play?" She had a strong accent.

"Sort of . . . Not really, I guess."

She laid her Israeli-style helmet on the table and her M-16 along the top of the booth backrest. Her dark brown hair was tied back in a bun. She had a full face, but it was pretty, with rosy cheeks, as if she'd pinched them that color, although he knew she hadn't. Everything about her was wholesome and natural.

Absently, trying hard not to stare at her, he strummed a chord.

"Do you mind if I listen?"

"Oh, hell's bells, of course not." He remembered himself and offered her one of the four beers he'd been rationed. "I'm Bobby Lee."

"Naarah."

It took him three tries to pronounce it even remotely like she had. But then he simpered and said, "It sounds pretty—even the way I mess it up."

She held the beer bottle with both hands. "Do you like fixing helicopters?"

"Love it." He took two quick sips. "You . . . you in the army?"

"Yes and no." Smiling, she shrugged.

"Yeah, well, I hear we had that kind of army ourselves back in the early seventies. That's before I got in."

"I mean . . . I am with the Nahal."

Bobby nodded as if he understood what she had said.

Then, after a thoughtful moment, he asked, "What's that?"

"The Pioneering Fighting Youth. A kind of national service."

He glanced at her M-16. "I'll say."

"We are trained to fight and farm. We set up—how do you say it—agri . . . agri . . ."

"Agriculture?"

"Yes," she laughed shyly. "That is it. We set up agriculture where it is more dangerous to have a usual kibbutz. Way up north, mostly."

"Just women?"

"Oh, no—there are men too."

Somehow he intuited that she didn't count a boyfriend among those men. "Are you on leave or something?"

"No, we came back to train. Mines."

"Laying or detecting?"

"Detecting."

Immediately, he saw in her eyes that something had happened recently. Something about mines she wasn't ready to talk about. "I'm sorry," he said.

She nodded, then smiled again. "Pardon me . . . my curiosity."

"Yeah?"

"Are you a cowboy?"

Bobby Lee chuckled. "No, honey, I'm a cracker."

Her forehead turned to wrinkles. "You mean like a biscuit?"

"No, like a hillbilly, a redneck, a hick?"

She still didn't understand.

"Okay, a cracker's a cowboy who's got a dirt-track Chevy instead of a horse. How's that?"

She giggled helplessly, her teeth very white in her deeply tanned face. "These words . . ."

"Let me put it this way, then. We believe in the same code as cowboys."

Her expression sobered. "Which is, Bobby?"

"Well . . ." All at once he felt self-conscious. But he went on. "You don't turn your back on folks who are in trouble, you never hurt somebody who can't defend hisself, especially women and kids—that's a humongous never."

"Even the families of your enemies?"

"I don't make war on families. I never have. I never will."

Her eyes had moistened. "I would like to live someplace where everybody honors such a code, Bobby."

He didn't know what to say, so he covered her hand with his.

Then an Israeli Air Force officer burst through the door and shouted something in what he supposed was Hebrew.

"What is it?" Bobby asked Naarah.

"Our plane"—she grabbed her helmet and rifle—"it is departing right away."

"Wait . . . where are you going? I mean, where are you based? Give me someplace I can write!"

"Nahal Golan." She had joined the others in the rush for the door.

"Where?" Bobby asked, following her, frisking his deep fatigue pants pockets for pen and paper, but finding only the ballpoint. "Here, write it on my hand."

Shouldering her M-16 with one hand and donning the helmet with the other, she scribbled something on Bobby's palm, then gently folded back his fingers, "Goodbye, Bobby Lee. God keep you safe."

McCoy halted him at the door. "That's far enough, hoss."

Disconsolately, he watched the line of young women jog out of sight. Then he held his palm up to the light. Looking confused, he showed it to the major. "Where the hell is this town?"

"It's not a town, Bobby. It's a word. *Shalom* means peace."

Bobby Lee stared off toward the flight line for a few seconds, then went back to his booth.

McCoy was shutting the doors to the Quonset, intending to bar them again, when a Huey with no markings dipped out of the sky in a half circle and landed in a storm of its own dust. A flight-suited crew chief jumped down and raced directly for him.

"Major McCoy?" he shouted over the whistling of the rotors.

"Yes!"

"You are to come with me, sir!"

Waiting inside the cabin were Nick Alexander and the Israeli from Mossad, Raffi Amir. As soon as McCoy was buckled down in a jump seat, the pilot lifted off.

"Please get comfortable, Major," Raffi said, raising his voice above the noise McCoy found all too familiar from Vienam.

"I take it you didn't make it up north tonight."

"No." Raffi pointed at the lights of a C-141 that was just lumbering onto a runway. "There goes my hop now. Nick and I received exceptional news during dinner. The chopper picked us up at a schoolyard down the road from my house—my little boy loves when that happens!"

"What news?"

"I will brief you along with someone else in but a few minutes. Otherwise, I will be repeating everything. A sign of old age, yes?"

McCoy sat back. Alexander had crossed his arms across his chest—his body language for feeling pretty smug. With the hand that Raffi couldn't see, he gave McCoy a thumbs-up sign.

Within a few minutes the urban glitter of Tel Aviv–Yafo sprawled into view through the open doors on both sides. The lights of beachfront high rises were reflected in magenta on the darkened Mediterranean. The pilot put the vintage UH-1 into a tank-killer dive, and the next thing McCoy knew they were flying down a canyon of modern skyscrapers, the variegated colors of office windows tunneling past like the climax to the movie *2001*.

These guys sure get the most out of their equipment, he thought to himself when the blood came back down off the vault of his cranium.

He had a glimpse of huge Hebraic characters on the side of the building the Huey was slowing to approach. "Mossad?" he asked Raffi, thinking that it might be the headquarters for the Israeli Central Institute for Intelligence and Special Missions, popularly known by the Hebrew word for "institute."

"No." Raffi looked amused., "Joseph Brothers International Textiles."

The Huey came to rest on one of two clearly marked helicopter pads in an expansive roof top compound. "What?"

"Let us say it is an *annex* of the Mossad. Welcome to Very Special Missions, gentlemen."

A young man, wearing a golf shirt and denims, was surveying a situation map, which McCoy quickly realized traced the entire odyssey of Flight 827.

"That will be all, thank you," Raffi dismissed him, then glanced at his watch. "It was necessary to call the Director away from a wedding—not his own, of course. In that case, we would have gone ourselves and whispered to him from behind the rabbi." His eyes darted to the ceiling. Another Huey could be heard thumping the air in approach to the roof. "Here he is now. I am sorry I will be unable to tell you his name. It is a state secret—even his wife is not supposed to know he is the Director of the Mossad. He answers only to the Prime Minister, and then maybe to his wife." Raffi seemed to be counting the stair steps down from the helicopter pads. Then he buttoned his coat, trying unsuccessfully to hide the pomegranate-juice stain in the crotch of his trousers.

A barrel-chested man of perhaps fifty hurtled himself through the double doors, wearing a skullcap over the crown of his honey-colored hair. He moved so decisively his pronounced limp did not seem like an impairment. "Nick Alexander?" he announced more than asked.

"Yes, sir"

"I want to shake your hand."

McCoy watched Alexander's normal-sized hand disappear inside the Director's bear paw. "My pleasure, sir."

"And this is his adjutant," Raffi said. "Major Scott McCoy."

"Good, good." In addition to an iron grip, the man had a penetrating stare. "Airborne" was his one-word verdict on McCoy.

"The Director," Raffi went on, "was a parachutist himself. He was also in on Entebbe."

"The planning, Amir, just the planning. And all because of this" Bending over, he used his knuckles to produce a knocking sound off his left foreleg. "This kept me from actually going to Uganda, and I curse the Syrian bastard who deprived me of Entebbe."

"I know the feeling," Alexander said.

The Director bobbed his head sympathetically. "Well, to be perfectly frank, Nick, I think your mission to Tehran was doomed from inception. The logistics! The distances!" He slapped his palm against his forehead. "But I admired your guts for trying. You showed the world just by trying. Now, Amir, what news?"

"The hostages have been located in West Beirut."

McCoy squeezed a fist shut behind his back.

"All of them?" the Director asked.

"Yes. And except for the ATW crew, the Americans are at essentially the same site—an Amal brigade headquarters and an adjoining Maronite school. We are already putting together maps and blueprints for the use of our American friends."

"Good . . . good. How old is your intelligence?"

"Four hours now."

"Not so good."

"This operative must work through the Phalangist network."

"Then we cannot communicate directly with him?"

"It is not practical at this point. And the Phalangist high command is a little piqued at us right now—for pulling out of Lebanon and leaving them to face the Moslems alone."

McCoy realized that the Director was studying him. The man's gaze then lit on Alexander briefly. "Excuse me, Nick, but let me ask your major what he thinks. He is the one with the big frown."

"I was about to ask him my self, sir."

"What do you say, Scott? No bullshitting now."

McCoy took a breath. "Your man may be one hell of an operative, but it's going to be our people with their butts on the line. I'd like to recon it myself."

"Good, good. Just what I would have said. But you don't look much like any Lebanese I have ever known. Your appearance is definitely North American, Major."

"How about a French Canadian then?"

"The idea has possibilities. I will leave you now to work out the details. Gentlemen . . ." The Director shook their hands. "Good luck to your Delta Force. And, Amir, if they need anything, see to it, yes?"

"Of course."

Then he bolted out through the double doors again, leaving McCoy feeling almost as if they'd been brushed off.

"Congratulations," Raffi said.

"For what?" Alexander looked as confused as McCoy felt.

"Excuse the Director's blunt manner—one does not get his job by being a withdrawn personality. The bottom line is that he has given you a carte blanche for whatever you even *think* you might require. A rare concession from this man, believe me."

"Anything?" Alexander asked.

"Try us."

"Well," McCoy half joked, "how about some intangible weaponry to slip past security at Beirut Airport?"

"Come," Raffi said without batting an eye.

On the way down to the basement of the building, Alexander and McCoy began roughing out a plan for the reconnaissance mission. "Take Peterson with you," the colonel said softly in the elevator. "You and he are the only two who are proficient in Arabic and French. Bobby Lee doesn't know it, and the French he speaks is called Cajun."

"I'll need a schedule of commercial flights into Beirut, boss."

"I am afraid that, after this hijacking," Raffi said, although he had been pretending not to eavesdrop, "there is only one carrier still willing to go there. The Lebanese one—Middle East Airlines. And they don't fly into Israel. You'll have to catch it from Cairo."

"Okay . . . thank you."

Alexander then said to the Israeli, "We're going to have to roll fast now that we have a fix on the hostages—if we don't want them packed up and moved on us."

"Most assuredly, Nick."

"How soon can my operators move up to the staging area?"

"While you conduct your business down here . . ." The elevator doors opened onto a laboratory, dark but for a single desk lamp under which a man in a white smock was eating his lunch. " . . . I will alert Haifa that Delta Force is on the way."

"We'd appreciate it."

"Shlomo, come here if you will." Quickly, Raffi explained what the Americans required, then withdrew to make his calls.

At first the technician seemed disgruntled for having his lunch break disturbed. But gradually he warmed to his subject. "The cretin who got himself captured in Athens?"

"Jaffar Ibn Khalil?" McCoy offered.

"Whatever. He bragged to the press that his buddies got their weapons through the machines by wrapping them in fiberglass insulation. Wrong. Pure camel shit. Even on anemic settings, a new scanner would still go off louder than three sevens in a row at Atlantic City." He smiled for the first time as he led them down an aisle between two long and cluttered workbenches. "I was born in Jersey. I should know. No, we both understand what happened at Athens Airport."

"Inside job?"

"Sure. That whole country's on the verge of going communist. Why the fuck not?" Halting before a steel door, he tried six keys before one worked. "Armory and range," he explained, flicking on a light and picking up what looked like a camera case from a shelf of various firearms. He continued to traipse along a musty corridor that eventually ended in a solitary shooting bench. He fumbled along the concrete wall for a second switch. Another light fifty feet down the firing lane revealed tiers of angled marine plate, designed to deflect and capture high-powered rounds. Opening the case, he took a few seconds to reacquaint himself with the contents, then quietly assembled a submachine gun from what had only moments before been harmless-looking camera components.

"All right, all right," Shlomo said. "What we have here is a .22-caliber high carbide glass SMG. The magazine holds 170 rounds of caseless hollow-point ammunition. The rate of fire is 600 rounds per minute. Weapon, magazine and ammunition are detection proof. One word of caution—there is no such thing as a wonder weapon. I don't give a crap what Ian Fleming wrote. To make this invisible to X-ray, we sacrificed durability. So don't go opening coconuts with it, okay? Here," he handed the featherweight piece to McCoy—"enjoy."

He glanced down the lane. "What do I shoot at?"

"Oh, hang on, hang on." Shlomo turned and pressed a button on a console.

As SAS-style silhouette lowered out of the ceiling.

"Wait." Shlomo had lifted his glasses onto his forehead while he squinted at the target. "That won't tell you anything." Hitting another button, he then smiled as a wooden frame containing some gray, opaque material descended into view. "Six inches of duct seal."

"Like what they used on ventilation equipment?" McCoy asked.

"Bingo. Better than anything else, it approximates the effect of bullets on human flesh. Shoot. Make a little blunt trauma. Come on, this is my lunch hour."

Not using the open sights, McCoy stared down the SMG's barrel with his dominant eye and let loose with a short burst.

Clearing the weapon, he followed Alexander up to the target.

The facing side of the chunk showed only a few disappointing pinpricks where the rounds had entered. Both men glanced behind the frame. Large cones in the claylike matter, six inches in diameter at their widest, showed where the rounds and much of the duct seal had exited. This missing material was now splattered over the steel plating behind them.

"It'll do," Alexander told the technician. "May we have two to go?"

"Hell, no, this is the only one in the world."

19 June 1985 . . . 1100 Hours . . . Beirut

"I am not a Jew!" The one called David Hoffman pounded the metal door with his fist one more time. "I attend Christian services at St. Catherine's Russian Orthodox Church in Chicago, Illinois." Slowly, his shoulder slid down the galvanized surface until he was slumping on the floor, his chest heaving with each loud sob.

The Roman Catholic priest left his mattress in the corner and tried to comfort the young man.

Benjamin Kaplan stared down at his own mattress. His fingers had almost worked free the stitching on a label that read *Property of Beirut Holiday Inn.*

"I am not a Jew," the man whimpered in the arms of the priest. "Father . . . Father, you must tell them that I am a Christian. My family . . . they have been Christians for centuries. Even against the communists . . . we remained faithful."

"Yes, my son, I know."

With a yank Benjamin removed the label, rolled it into a ball and flicked it away. His son, Robert, was finally sleeping—that was good.

All at once Hoffman and the priest were sprawling on the concrete floor six feet away from the door, which had been forced open against their weight.

Standing one pace inside the basement chamber, the light from the corridor spilling around him, Abdul asked, "Who carries on so?"

"I'm sorry," Hoffman said, rising to his knees, "I was simply explaining that I am not a Jew. So shouldn't I be confined with the other Gentiles? Shouldn't I have the comfort of my own kind?"

The terrorist nodded as if he understood perfectly.

"Very well, I will see to it you have your comfort."

"Oh, thank you"

Ambling forward, Abdul drew his now familiar silver pistol from his waistband and held it to Hoffman's forehead. His forefinger slid around the trigger. He waited while Hoffman trembled helplessly, expecting his life to end in an explosion.

But then, smirking, Abdul lowered the weapon to his side and said into the man's bulging eyes, "What you feel at this moment is great comfort, yes?"

Hoffman spun away from Abdul's shoes and retched.

"Now you will cause no more disturbances. Otherwise, I will indeed kill you." He walked out, bolting the door before he could be heard strolling down the passageway.

"Do you see now?" Benjamin asked quietly.

Drying his mouth with his sleeve, Hoffman gaped at him in silence.

"See?" Benjamin went on. "You are not a Jew by blood or religion or even conviction. Today, this hour, you are a Jew because they insist that you be one. So, young man, your denials are pointless."

Hoffman clung to the priest again. "Father, I do not wish to die."

"I know, but we must not fear death. Death is not so terrible as long as we—"

"You are a good man, Father. I am sure of it," Benjamin interrupted. "And I should not presume to talk about what you believe. The truth is, I don't know if I understand what you believe. So, instead, let me tell you what I learned from the worst times of my life . . ." He smiled wearily at his son, who was now sitting upright, his usually smooth face darkened by a week's growth of beard. ". . . times I have never discussed even with those I love most." He met the eyes of the other Jews who were squatting on their mattresses: *No, I can tell in an instant—none of them were there.* "Anxiety . . . how long have we been living with it now? Six days? Sixty? A lifetime? But as bad as this feeling of terror becomes, do not imagine that death is any better! Never!" Realizing that he had raised his voice, he smiled for a moment. "Close friends—Jews and Gentiles alike who learned that I had been in a camp—have asked me how all those people could go like sheep to their executions. What were they feeling that they could behave so?" He squeezed his eyelids shut, then opened them again. "Relief! Yes, that was it! At last they were being rescued from that awful anxiety that seemed like it would go on forever—even though they were being rescued only by extinction! So, my friends, as long as we remain in the hands of these bullies, we must not discuss death as if it were a friend. We must resist it. We must despise it. Agreed?"

Roger Campbell blinked into the strong sunlight, his eyes burning. Jaffar had trapped the back of his head with a pistol so many times there was now a sore, puffy spot there. He wanted to grab the handgun and fling it out the open side window. But he resisted the urge. It was suicidal, a clearer voice said from deep within his weariness. Would that voice eventually become a faint echo, and then desert him entirely? "Captain!" one of the newsmen shouted for his attention from down on the apron. "How are you and your crew being treated?"

Looking askance, Campbell saw Dave Hoskins, his flight engineer, slumped forward in his seat, elbows on his knees, drawn face clasped between his fingers. A Russian-made rifle was being held against his neck by one of three militiamen who had remained aboard with Jaffar. After his failure in Athens, he felt the need to be twice as cruel and unpredictable as Abdul and Mustafa had been.

Campbell struggled to smile for the cameras. It was for his aged parents. Thinking of them, he swore eternal vengeance if this thing affected the health of either one of them. "We are being treated well—all of us are well."

"Do you want to go home?"

No, you stupid fuckhead, I want to apply for Lebanese citizenship and run for local imam in the next election. Campbell tried to turn away from the sun, but Jaffar's pistol prevented any movement. "I hope all of us . . . all the people on my flight . . . get home soon. You bet."

"Is there anything you need?"

"No. We're being given everything we require."

The reporters began elbowing each other to break free of the ever-growing throng and holler their questions at him. "Is it true the Jewish passengers have been segregated from the others? How many people have been killed by the hijackers so far? What do you think of reported plans for U.S. military intervention in . . . ?"

Two rounds went off close to Campbell's face. Instinctively, he ducked down.

"Away!" Jaffar was screaming at the reporters. He fired in their direction once more. "All of you—being away at once!"

Then the pistol was jabbing against Campbell's sore spot again.

Ed Jones was startled out of his sleep by something slapping against the floor. He rolled over, awakening Andy, who was lying the other way on the only mattress in the cell.

Both of them stared up at Abdul, who was smiling at them.

"What time is it?" Ed asked, rising on an elbow.

"Time for American news magazines."

There was a copy of *Newsweek* on the floor.

"Thanks."

"Do not mention it." Abdul left them.

The instant the door clicked shut, the Marines dived for the magazine, both of them seizing it at the same time, nearly tearing off the cover in the process. "Easy, dude."

"Eddy, look! The cover! We're news!"

"Of course we're news. We're probably the biggest news in the world right now. Page eight—easy now."

Sitting side by side, they turned to the story. Ed resolved to read the lead paragraph first, but his eyes were automatically drawn to the black-and-white photograph on the opposite page.

A night scene. Looked like an airport. A perimeter of Arab soldiers in the background. Something under a poncho.

Telling himself to calm down, he ran a trembling finger underneath the caption: *"Body of murdered U.S. Marine dumped on tarmac at Algiers Airport."*

Ed shot to his feet. He began pacing around the cubicle. But pacing was not enough. He picked up the chamber pot and hurled it against the iron grille over the high window. But that was not enough either.

Then he burst into tears. "They didn't even know him, Andy. Those motherfuckers didn't even know him!"

1200 Hours . . . Cairo

McCoy found it impossible to sleep.

But he might not have another opportunity for forty-eight hours—or longer. Not only Delta, but American military units all over the Mediterranean—and the world, actually—were waiting on the message he would send from Beirut. So he disciplined himself and stretched out on a bench inside the noisy Cairo terminal as Peterson had done.

Peter, true to form, had thrown an arm over his eyes

and was out cold, his breath buzzing in his adenoids.

They and the other passengers on the Middle East Airlines flight had already boarded and deplaned once without having ever left the ground. McCoy and Peterson had just buckled themselves in when a German businessman brought it to the attention of a stewardess that fuel was trickling out of the starboard wing of the aged Boeing 707. "It is of no importance," she told him, then went for the flight engineer. "It is of little importance," he said with a smile, then sent for the pilot, who announced a delay until "a condensation problem of minor importance" in the wing could be repaired.

"N'importe pas," Peterson sighed, keeping in character with the French-Canadian covers they had assumed upon departing from Ben-Gurion International Airport.

McCoy had found himself almost wishing that they had infiltrated by land, although Raffi had told them that passing through Shia southern Lebanon would have tested their cover stories to the maximum, especially for two light-complexioned men. Waukene would have been a natural for this covert operation, but his inventory of foreign languages included neither French not Arabic. Peterson had mastered Farsi for the Tehran raid and, in the past few years, had developed a working knowledge of Arabic. McCoy could sometimes understand what was said to him —but only if the words were pronounced the way his Saudi instructor had spoken them.

The two operators filed back into the terminal with the other passengers. They killed time by wandering through the duty-free shops. In a way it reminded McCoy of their Vietnam days together, shopping in Saigon or speaking nothing but French all night at Papa Emile's place over an endless amber stream of cognac. Papa Emile, his gentle-voiced Montagnard wife, their Highlands coffee plantation, the Special Forces camp overlooking the gorgeous greens of their estate—all swept away by the Tet offensive.

Finally McCoy slept. But it was a gray sleep, too close to consciousness to be restful.

Peterson shook him awake, scaring him half to death. He told him in French that they finally had a departure.

McCoy sat up, hyperventilating for a moment. Bad dreams. *"Quelle heure est-il?"*

"C'est midi."

"Merde . . . déjà?"

They bantered in French all the way into Lebanese airspace. Upper Michigan abounded in transplanted *Canadiens,* so McCoy felt he had the accent down pretty well, and he now worked to get the Viet inflection out of Peterson's French. It kept his mind off other things.

But then, without giving a reason, the pilot announced that the landing would be delayed a few minutes. A few minutes became an hour. McCoy and Peterson grew increasingly restless. Something was happening at the airport, and McCoy hoped it wasn't Flight 827 warming up for one more departure—to Iran, which would change the entire scope of the game.

Finally McCoy flagged down the stewardess and confided in her that his friend and he were newspeople for a rather hefty network . . .

"Télévision?" she asked hopefully.

"Oui . . ." And they were wondering if she might tell them, confidentially of course, what was happening on the ground at Beirut International.

Peterson began examining her face from different angles.

Giving him her best side, she whispered that, earlier today, one of the hijackers had opened fire on some newsmen standing near the ATW plane. The tower had forbidden any traffic to land until the incident was fully resolved, although she was not sure what that meant, other than more circling for the Middle East Airlines flight.

She cautioned McCoy and Peterson to be careful

while in Beirut. Rumor had it that the crazy Americans were going to invade any hour.

"*Merci,*" McCoy murmured.

"Canadian?" The Lebanese customs officer glanced at the red-maple-leaf pin on McCoy's lapel as he reached for his passport.

"*Oui, Canadien—CBC.*"

"*Ah, bien.*" He babbled on about television crews coming from all over the world to Beirut, as he stamped McCoy's passport. Then, after thumbing through Peterson's folder just for drill, he told the men to proceed.

McCoy and Peterson removed their camera cases and placed them on the conveyer belt. They glided inside the hand-baggage scanner. The case containing the components of the .22-caliber submachine gun was ignored, but the guard motioned for Peterson to open his.

The Lebanese had a Smith & Wesson wheel-gun on his hip.

"What is in this?" He had opened an aluminum can. In it was one of the lenses to the disassembled night-vision goggles.

"*Pardon, monsieur?*"

"*Qu'est-ce que ceci?*"

Peterson coughed into his hand, stalling for time while trying to think of the words for video camera lens.

McCoy wasn't sure either, but he improvised. "*Un objectif pour le video-cam.*"

"*Bon . . . merci.*"

McCoy stepped through the metal detector, smiling at the Lebanese Forces soldier who was carefully scrutinizing everyone who passed within range of his M-16. The man did not smile back.

And then McCoy steeled himself. The alarm was buzzing, and Peterson had halted a step beyond the machine, holding up his palms in surprise.

The soldier grasped the T-bar of his rifle, and the

guard ordered Peterson to empty everything in his pockets on a tray. The biggest single item was a Sony Walkman radio-cassette player. *"Pour le jazz,"* he explained, simulating the headphones by plugging his ears with his fingertips as he passed through the machine a second time, emerging clean.

Without a word the guard returned Peterson's possessions to him.

The operators sauntered on down the concourse. Peterson still clutched the Sony as if it were the most valuable radio in the world at this moment. Perhaps it was, McCoy thought, winking at his partner, who exhaled in a loud rush of breath. *"Merde, baby."*

"What was that *pour le jazz* crap?"

"I couldn't think of the word for jogging. Besides, I didn't hear you jumping in to help."

After claiming their luggage, their first task was to recon the area where Flight 827 had come to rest. A loose cordon of Lebanese Forces turned them back at one point, explaining in Arabic that the hijackers were shooting newsmen today—despite the fact that McCoy and Peterson spoke only in French to them.

Next the operators located a stairwell. The door providing access to it—and the roof above—was locked. McCoy examined the lock-in-knob device, then whispered, "Piece of cake."

Retiring to a stall in the men's restroom, he removed his set of picks from his grooming kit.

In two minutes they were on the roof of the main terminal building, keeping to the shadow thrown by the taller tower structure, whose summit was sandbagged and manned by two Lebanese troops who were virtually unconscious as they traded a pair of binoculars back and forth for peeks at women waiting for taxis down on Avenue de L'Aeroport.

Also to the immediate north was the expanse of dirt where the Marine headquarters building had stood. *All those guys,* McCoy thought, *and it's like they never died there, for all anybody cares around here.*

Reaching the parapet on the southern line of the roof, McCoy and Peterson spent five minutes memorizing the layout: the 727, vehicles parked near it, the closest available cover and concealment, and the positions of the Lebanese Army—which would probably take no action against any American response, but nevertheless had to be taken into account as a potential hostile force. From this vantage, McCoy couldn't see inside the cockpit, and all the hatches on the aircraft were sealed.

"Okay, Pete," McCoy said softly, "let's go jump through the next hoop."

Waiting in the passenger loading zone on Avenue de L'Aeroport, the operators started a heated argument with each other over whether to use a taxi or a bus to get inside Beirut. This was to give Peterson a chance to get a better look at the two Arabs in grimy T-shirts who had fallen in behind them near a newsstand inside the terminal. The diversion also gave McCoy an opportunity to furtively check out the column of vehicles, cabs mostly, parked along the curb.

Turning away as if at the end of his patience with Peterson, he flagged down the first taxi in line. Before it could reach where the operators stood waiting, the battered cab was cut off by an ambulance. The hack driver laid on his horn, but the four white-garbed attendants ignored him as they poured out of the emergency vehicle —and began firing their Kalashnikov rifles into the air.

One of them screamed in French for the operators to get inside—or die on the spot.

Still clutching their luggage, slack-jawed and flatfooted, McCoy and Peterson were jostled into the ambulance, which immediately pulled away, siren wailing. To discourage any potential witnesses, the man in the shotgun seat fired a burst along a stone retaining wall. Everyone within a hundred-meter radius went prone, as if they'd executed this evasive movement a hundred times before.

Beirut, McCoy thought to himself.

One of the gunmen was staring at him.

McCoy stared back at him.

Within a quarter mile the siren was shut down, having done a nice job of clearing the traffic thus far. The tires screaked as the driver cut the rig sharply around a corner. The side road gently climbed up onto a plateau covered with broken patches of scrub. Houses, many of them bombed out, were scattered here and there in the rolling hills to the east.

"This is it," the driver said in English, braking hard as he pulled into a turn-out near an olive orchard. The crescent of dirt was littered with spent 155mm casings, the brass scintillated by the sun—American tax dollars slowly turning green again in the marine air. McCoy frowned.

The ambulance was still rolling to a stop when a Ford cargo van pulled out of concealment inside the orchard.

The vehicles came to rest side by side.

"Go!" the driver told McCoy and Peterson. "Quickly!"

The rear door to the van had already been cracked open for them. Hands reached out for their luggage.

"Merci," McCoy said, crawling into the van behind Peterson.

Immediately, both vehicles sped away from the turn-out, the ambulance streaking south along an unpaved lane and the van north along an improved road that was more potholes than asphalt—toward Beirut's chipped and broken skyline.

The car radio was turned low to an Arabic-speaking station.

The high-backed front passenger seat swiveled around, and a uniformed man in middle-age confronted the Americans. He said nothing for a moment, his face humorless. Around his neck, partially covering a burn scar that ran up his jawline to a shriveled ear, was the jaunty red and gold scarf of the Italian Marines. But this soldier was not a member of any peacekeeping force.

"I will not tell you my name," he finally said in excellent English. "I cannot extend to you the hospitality of my headquarters." A hint of a smile came to his mouth, rippling the scar. "There are two reasons for my bad manners. Firstly, as a dear teacher once told me, for every action there is an opposite and equal reaction. So it is with Beirut. I have just described the condition of my country in a nutshell. I want no Shia reprisals for helping you as little as I am." Glancing forward through the windshield, he recommended a different road to the driver, who nodded and turned without slowing in the least. "Secondly," the man went on, "I have every expectation that, given the present excitement in our city, both of you will be in Amal's hands before the sun rises again."

"We were being followed at the airport," McCoy said. "Was it the Shi'ites?"

"Of course it was—and probably the Syrians were there too. Perhaps even some Palestinians. All keeping watch for the American agents everyone fully expects to arrive before a full-scale military intervention takes place —what, tomorrow, the day after?"

Neither operator said anything.

"But we anticipated that these people would be at the airport. That is why we told the Israelis we insisted on this little scene at the airport. In Beirut everyone must be accounted for. Now the Amal agents will report back that —" He paused, leaning his good ear toward the radio. "Turn it up."

McCoy could see that the announcer's lightning pace was frustrating Peterson's comprehension.

The man threw back his head and laughed as if in self-congratulation. "Someone reportedly from the Awali River Marxist Popular Front has just phoned the station. His group claims responsibility for the kidnapping of two Canadian journalists who were, in reality, CIA spies." He waved for his driver to turn it off. "So now you two strangers have been accounted for. That is what the Amal men will report back to my old friend, Georges. You will be forgotten for a short while. We are entering the city. Please stay down."

The driver turned to the right. Through the tinted top of the windshield, McCoy could see nothing but the partially collapsed face of an office building, and he wondered if a collision was imminent. But then the van nosed down and entered the darkness of an underground parking level.

"Do you need a map of the city?" the man asked.

"No," McCoy said.

"Good. The Green Lines lies two blocks west of here. I suggest that you cross after nightfall. And I demand this —do not attempt to contact our operative at the site. He has already endangered himself too much for the sake of your hostages. It would be a different thing if you Americans intended to stay in Lebanon. But you don't have the stomach for that, do you? You have proved yourselves to be fickle allies, yes? So any risks we take in your behalf are pointless, tactically speaking." In the echoing subterranean darkness, he chuckled again. "Besides, I have a fondness for this operative. After all, he taught me all the angles. In Christ's name, good luck."

"Wait," McCoy asked from the cement, "can you loan us some firepower—even a handgun?"

"I am sorry. You will soon learn—there are no secrets in Beirut. I do not want it said that I armed two American agents."

The van spun around and accelerated for the daylight.

Picking up their luggage, McCoy and Peterson moved for the shadows.

21

2100 Hours . . . Beirut

There was only one way to do it.

Peterson's eyes shone in his darkly camouflaged face. He agreed; McCoy recognized the look. He also knew the pigheaded expression when the sergeant major *didn't* agree.

There was no way to cross Rue de Damas without exposing themselves for the first twenty meters. No matter how well you planned an infiltration, this sort of thing just couldn't be avoided sometimes, like broken legs and ambushes.

The Green Line at this point consisted of a split-level boulevard, the eastern two lanes ten feet higher than the western, which were so choked with growth they looked more like a *barranca* in El Salvador than half of a *rue* in what at one time had been called "the Paris of the Middle East."

McCoy and Peterson would cross at the same time, matching each other stride for stride. Going at intervals was a good way to get the second man gunned down. Even had ten operators been along tonight, facing the same open expanse of roadway, they still would have team-rushed across, hoping to catch any sniper unawares with his bolt open and his trigger finger two knuckles up his noses. Thankfully, there wasn't much electricity left in this part of town, and the distant sign above a Toyota dealership had only two letters lit—the rest had been shot out.

McCoy and Peterson looked each other over, making sure all their gear was securely fastened to their body harnesses.

McCoy grasped the SMG with both hands. "Why not?"

That was the signal. They sprinted across the pavement, then spider-crawled over the embankment wall and dropped noisily into West Beirut.

McCoy chose nothing that even vaguely resembled a path through the chest-high weeds. He had learned from Raffi Amir that this gorge of slime and debris had been mined by both sides numerous times during the past decade. Once he froze, thinking that he'd run up against a trip wire. But it proved to be a downed telephone line. Another gold star for the low-cut soft shoes the team had adopted for covert situations. Bobby Lee sneeringly called them *ball-et* slippers, but in addition to being quiet, they gave an operator's feet greater sensitivity to feel things—almost like a second pair of hands. Walking on the sides of those shoes now, McCoy eased across a trickle of scummy waters.

Peterson and he were almost through the shattered front of a department store when a machine gun—an old Browning, McCoy was sure—began barking mindlessly at the night. Peterson and he leaped behind a jumble of broken concrete.

It took only seconds for them to realize that the fire wasn't being directed against them. If the news footage McCoy had seen of Beirut street action was any indication, the long bursts were only some heavily armed town crier's way of broadcasting that it was nine o'clock and all was .50 caliber.

"Shit," Peterson whispered.

They sifted through the ruins of the department store to the next narrow *rue*—then had to withdraw to the tilting second story because a squad of militiamen was working the street level, clearing dark areas the old-fashioned way: *by shooting into them.*

When he finally did retire, McCoy decided, he wanted the ammunition concession in Lebanon. There was never a five-minute period in which somebody somewhere wasn't busting caps. Already it had become white noise to him.

The next street they reached was even crazier. Old men were sitting on the sidewalk in a space they'd cleared of broken concrete and twisted reinforcing bars. Someone had an accordion going, and two old duffers were reeling around each other. At the end of the block seventy-five meters away, a teenage kid was manning a rubble barricade, peeking over its top, looking for something to blow up with his RPG-7. The corner grocery market to his back was open for business; a friend brought him out a Coke.

"This is going to take more time than we thought." Peterson scanned the smashed-out windows of the buildings opposite them with the night-vision goggles. "*Beaucoup* more time than we thought."

"There are damn near a million people in this burg —and I'll bet half of them are packing heat tonight. See anything?"

"Yup—we got a sniper down the block. Third story."

"Okay, let's detour around him."

It was eleven o'clock before they reached the beach on the westernmost edge of Beirut, and then another half hour elapsed before they had a view of Mt. Lebanon Maronite Church and School—after Peterson had nearly walked into the swimming pool of an abandoned luxury resort. The black waters were so thick with dross and refuse they had looked like a trashy but solid surface to the operator through the night-vision equipment.

Suppressing laughter, McCoy caught him by the arm just before he took the plunge.

"You take the point then, asshole," Peterson hissed.

"Shit, no—we're getting into Indian territory."

"Don't let Winnemucca hear you say that."

They surveyed the school from an apartment balcony for a few minutes, but then decided to push forward to the rocky point on which the Maronite facility stood. Only from there could they fully see the Amal brigade headquarters.

"On the bank above the beach . . . straight ahead,"

Peterson said, flipping up the goggles to see the area in natural rather than enhanced starlight, "they've got a sentry."

"We'll just have to work around him."

"That means we get wet, because there're two more on the high ground with a light machine gun."

"Big fucking deal, Peter."

The waters were pleasantly warm, and the swells no more than a foot high as they waded up to the armpits through the Mediterranean. They remained ten meters out from the shoreline but worked parallel to it, over a bottom of slippery rocks.

Unsure what brine would do to the carbide glass SMG, McCoy held it above his head.

Suddenly Peterson went under. McCoy grabbed for him with his free hand—but came up empty.

Then, ten feet ahead, the sergeant major breached the surface, foam trickling off his black watchcap and water filling the bottom half of each goggle.

"Find a little hole?" McCoy whispered.

They lay in their wet jump suits behind a spur of wave-sanded rock. It was McCoy's turn to look at the world in greenish starlight.

Now he understood what the operative had meant by "poles everywhere." The militiamen had ripped up enough pipe to irrigate a small city and stuck the ten-foot lengths in every flat piece of ground near the headquarters and the school. This was a tactic borrowed, no doubt, from the Iranian Revolutionary Guards, who'd done the same to the compound of the American Embassy in Tehran—all to prevent rescue helicopters from landing. McCoy smiled as he wondered if any IRG had volunteered to help their Shi'ite brothers here in Lebanon. *All the sweeter,* he thought as he redirected his attention on four barrels jutting skyward out of a vineyard south of the headquarters building.

"Pete, if I said four 23mm cannon, what would you say?"

"I'd say Russian ZSU-23-4 self-propelled antiaircraft gun."

"That's what I thought." McCoy shook his head. It was an impressive weapon: a light armored chassis boasting four computer-directed cannon. This one was dug in, which was pure stupidity. The system's biggest plus was its mobility. Still, it was death to any helicopter within range. This, the thicket of poles bristling skyward, the contempt he felt for choppers as the main reason for the Desert One catastrophe—all combined to tell him that Delta Option One, insertion by Sixth Fleet Sea Stallions, was a no-go.

Option Two was equally absurd: a parachute jump into the site. With the sea on one side and the jagged wreckage of West Beirut on the other, that was a recipe for an instant twenty-percent casualty rate. Quite simply, Delta could not hope to free the hostages with seven fewer operators. It was going to be tight enough with all thirty-six men in one piece when the starting flag went down.

Option Three, direct assault by landing craft, still had possibilities. But before McCoy made up his mind, he wanted to have a look inside the gun port of the old bunker he had spotted beneath a canopy of camouflage netting. There was also a sewer pipe to inspect.

He crawled forward. Peterson followed without a word.

Abdul knocked on the door.

"Come in, come in."

Georges was seated behind a large desk. The light from a lamp was reflecting off a snow-white page he was reading, illuminating his face from below, making it seem more paltry than usual. The expensive carpet, the delicately carved wooden screen panels hiding the window at Georges's back, made Abdul feel uncomfortable. It was all too opulent for the severity of his convictions. At his barracks in the Bekaa Valley, he and his comrades slept on the floor, ate at plywood tables, ran bare-chested even in the snow.

In that moment, while Georges continued to read, Abdul realized that, like many of the bourgeois moderates in Iran's preliminary revolutionary government, this man with soft hands and gold chains under his silk shirt would not live to grow a gray beard. It was good that Georges had already made his pilgrimage to Mecca.

"Thank you for coming so promptly, my brother." Georges took off his reading glasses and rubbed his bloodshot eyes. "How go the defensive measures?"

"Well enough—although these things should have been done days ago."

"Yes, yes. Well, situations change quite rapidly, don't they? And we must flow with them. I am the kind of man who is always open to suggestion—"

"What has happened?" Abdul cut him short. "You did not summon me to hear what kind of man you are."

Instead of becoming angry, Georges massaged his temples with his fingertips. His voice was a rasp. "Today, after the talks, a trusted friend with the Syrian mission, he slipped me an extraordinary intelligence document in a book of poems by Gibran, a gift. This report was intended only for President Assad's eyes. Yet, probably believing my life to be at stake, this brother risked everything to make sure I received a copy. Penciled in the margin here, he begs me to share this information with no one else. He will be disgraced, even shot if—"

"Then why do you tell me, Georges?"

The man lowered his eyes. "You cannot imagine the burden of knowing these things. I will need help to see that certain measures are adopted immediately."

Abdul glared at him. "Tell me—everything."

"The deplorable attempt by the Algerians to free the hostages . . ."

"Yes?"

"It was only a cover. No Algerians were directly involved. The American counterterrorist unit, Delta Force, conducted the entire operation."

"Did I not tell everyone that? I said the commandos were Americans, not Algerians. It was you, Georges, who chose to believe the Algerian president's lie and disregard the truth I shared with you."

"We must not quarrel, my brother. Now, this I find to be significant . . ." Georges slipped on his glasses again. " 'The Soviets inform us (most probably on the basis of reports from their Mediterranean fleet) that this U.S. extraordinary operations group was equipped with state-of-the-art communications apparatus: specifically, field transceivers that can interface directly with military satellites. This enabled them to enjoy a remarkable quality of communication between all levels of command on an instantaneous basis . . .' "

"So?" Abdul asked. "What does this matter to us?"

"There is more. Believe me, it all comes together in a most disturbing way." The page vibrated in Georges's grasp. " 'Within minutes after the unsuccessful operation, an HC-130 Hercules tactical transport was observed by a friendly operative departing from the Algiers airport. This aircraft was tracked by the Soviets to the western extremity of Israeli airspace, at which time Israeli ECM—' "

"What is this thing?"

"Electronic countermeasures. It confounds radar, you see. Quite simply, the American plane disappeared inside Israel."

Abdul fell silent for a moment. He sensed an opportunity for Hizbollah—and perhaps for himself in Georges's waning self-confidence. He would not press the man so hard.

The Amal leader read on: " 'The Soviets were able to identify the two frequencies on which the Americans communicated during the Algiers operation. Sensitive to legitimate Syrian interests in Lebanon, the Soviets have offered to make available these frequencies to our own ECM unit, presently based near Sofar in the Shouf Mountains.' "

"Has this been done?" Abdul took out his nickel-plated Beretta, polished its barrel with his sleeve, then returned the pistol to his waistband.

Georges was still staring at the weapon as he said, "I don't know. There was no way I could ask without jeopardizing my friend's life."

"Then what measures are you suggesting we take here in Beirut?"

"We must adapt our thinking to the new situation. You took Flight 827 to Algiers—and the Americans followed. You have brought the hostages to Beirut—and now the Americans are within striking distance from Israel. And this radio equipment—quite obviously it permits that . . . that trigger-happy President of theirs to personally direct these raids from the White House. I tell you, that man is a cowboy. He loves this sort of thing!"

Abdul thought to ask Georges why, only a few short hours ago, he had not been overly concerned about the intentions of the American President in the least. But he decided not to. He realized that he and Hizbollah had already won; Georges and Amal were beaten. In the interests of Arab unity, it was best to remain quietly gracious.

"Tell me what you want done," Abdul said, rising, "and we shall do it together."

Georges bolted to his feet, clapped his hands together, then came around the desk to peck Abdul on both cheeks. "Thank you, my brother. I had no doubt I could reply on you. This way I can devote my full energies to the negotiations here in Beirut."

"While I do what?"

"Why, Abdul, have you forgotten your own suggestion—to take the hostages to Bekaa?"

"Frankly, yes, in my press of duties here."

"Well, give the word immediately to our people.

The hostages must leave as soon as possible."

"Tonight?"

"Of course. We must have darkness to get them safely over the mountains. And trucks. See if some brothers in Lebanese Forces can be persuaded to defect tonight with some trucks."

Turning, Abdul said, "I will see to it that your orders are executed without delay."

He was smirking as he went through the door, for Georges was still mumbling to himself. "And more forces, I will summon more volunteers from the militia units in the south . . ."

With the aid of the goggles, McCoy could clearly see through the embrasure of the bunker. But no weapon was visible within, and in over ten minutes only once did a human shape pass across the narrow slit—a man rose, then sat again.

Peterson tapped him on the shoulder, then communicated to him in a series of hand signals. They had talked to each other this way over so many years, during so many operations, the gestures had become idiomatic. Peterson was going to take a gander inside the concrete structure, and he wanted the goggles. McCoy began to hand him the SMG as well, but the sergeant major waved off the offer. Then, before crawling forward, he grinned at McCoy and rested his left hand on top of the erect middle finger of his right hand: *Cover me, I'm fucked.*

Peterson's stealth was close to being artistry. He flowed along as part of the terrain, the shadows, the night itself. He could mesmerize even the keenest eye into believing that he was not there. The other operators had ribbed him about it, but he'd spent a lot of time watching nature films on the big cats, stopping the projector as he noted each infinitesimal aspect of movement. Bobby Lee was the only operator not to tease Peterson about his tiger movies; he'd get a cup of coffee and join the sergeant major in the darkened room. *Wild Kingdom* was his favorite show.

McCoy smiled as he quickly made a bed check on the silhouetted militiamen within a hundred meters of the bunker. Not one in ten of them was on his toes.

The operative, whoever he was, had done a good piece of Humint on this place. He must have had some decent training; his intelligence report had zeroed in on the same things that now concerned McCoy. The sewer pipe outlet directly behind him reportedly provided tight but adequate ingress to the basement of the headquarters. Given the time constraints, there was no way to test that assumption at the moment, but he was willing to bet that the operative knew what he'd been talking about—or the fact wouldn't have been included in his IR. It'd be nice to talk to the agent, but it wasn't worth getting him snuffed by Amal.

Peterson slid in beside him again, and signaled that he wanted to withdraw some distance to talk. He grasped his hand to his throat to indicate that it had something to do with the hostages.

Near the soughing of the waves again, he whispered, "They're going to pull the old shell game on us, Scottie."

"When?"

"Sounds like ASAP—before dawn if they can get the transportation together. And that's not the worst of it. I overheard somebody inside the bunker say Bekaa."

"Shit." Amal's bundling the Americans off to the Bekaa Valley would change the entire scope of the operation. The most dangerous radicals in the Middle East were conveniently garrisoned at two or three sites in that region of eastern Lebanon, but Washington would probably balk at taking action against them there. Bekaa was under the de facto control of Syria. If inserted into this Valley of the Shadow, Delta would most certainly have to clash with Syrian troops. In addition to pitting the operators against heavy armor—which was beyond their purpose and capabilities as a unit, this might draw Syria's ally, the Soviet Union, into the fray.

World War Three on tomorrow night's eleven o'clock news.

As soon as he'd dropped this bomb, Peterson hurriedly explained that he'd seen five militiamen inside the bunker, squatting on the floor, smoking and drinking tea around a candle.

Also inside was a Russian 57mm antitank gun that could be swung up into the embrasure at a moment's notice. The bunker would then become a fanatic's fun zone, a three-sided shooting gallery on the Mediterranean.

So Option Three, direct amphibious assault on the site, was looking as grim as One and Two. This was neither the time nor the place to reenact Tarawa. "And Scottie, two of the bastards inside don't speak Arabic any better than I do."

"Farsi?"

"You bet. It's through these Iranians I understood most of what's going down in a few hours. And everybody was talking about Shiraz like it's their alma mater."

This Iranian city, McCoy recalled, was where Khomeini's Revolutionary Guard trained the suicide squads that were then disseminated throughout the unsuspecting Moslem world.

"Okay, Peter, it's time we start exfiltrating. But first I got a person-to-person call to dial." He removed the Sony Walkman from a pouch in his jump suit, donned the headset and pulled out the rewind button, which became an external antenna. "Little Boss to Big Boss . . . hello . . ." He heard nothing but crazy undulations of static, manic squeals that made him grit his teeth. "Hey, Boss . . . you got your ears on?"

"You getting anything?"

McCoy ripped off the headset and handed it to Peterson. "Listen to this."

After a moment, Peterson asked, "Do you think our little swim messed up the circuitry?"

"It's supposed to be waterproof. If you could breathe, you'd be able to talk under water with the son of a bitch. No, hello Russia—only they could do this." He tried one last time, then groaned and put the satellite transceiver away. "Any ideas?"

"Yeah, one. The Phalangist operative has to have a radio."

"He might. But what happens if he tells us to go fish?"

"We're no worse off than we are now."

"We could try to get to our temporary embassy out at Baabda."

Peterson glanced at the dim phosphorescence of his watch dial. "That's at least ten klicks away. And dressed in these black duds, I'd shoot us myself if I were a Marine gatekeeper. If you're thinking Option Four like I am, Delta has to leave Haifa in the next hour or we'll never even come close to stopping the bastards from highballing our people to Bekaa."

McCoy exhaled: Peterson was right. This option, the only realistic one now, called for an amphibious landing eight miles down the coast on the sandy beach between the airport and the Lebanese Army–held village of Khalde, then a breakneck convoy to the objectives inside Beirut. "I'll give us twenty minutes to locate the operative. Then we've got no choice. We've got to think of something else."

"I'll bet he's not inside Amal headquarters."

"You *hope* he isn't. We really don't have a clue who this guy is."

As they stole toward the Maronite buildings, McCoy had a ghastly vision straight out of *Dr. Strangelove* with himself trying to place a collect long-distance call through an Arabic-speaking Lebanese telephone operator to the President of the United States. The mental image might have almost seemed funny had he not been as close to tension sickness as he had ever come in his life.

Besides, every public telephone he had seen in West

Beirut had been shot dead right between the finger holes. The people here seemed to hate telephones as much as they hated one another.

Peterson halted him with a hand signal. They had a sentry to get around.

22

20 June 1985 . . . 0005 Hours

The Countenance.

It was both familiar and eternally fresh. When strong sunlight streamed across his beatific face, he appeared to be very resolute—a leader among men, a warrior priest. But in flickering candlelight, as now, his stained-glass features looked meditative, belonging to a seeker of quiet truths.

Saint Maron. The hermit monk.

Long ago, when Brother John had had enough of taverns and bordellos raucous with soldiers, he had dreamed of a hermitage like Maron's in the mountains of Apamea. But a life of contemplation had not been ordained for him; he had remained among men all these years of service. And when one remains in the world of men, one must constantly make choices. He must have a durable faith that can weather unavoidable compromises. Still, Brother John had no doubt that he had served God and his people well. When possible, he had also tried to serve the cause of peace among all men.

But now, this night, he knew he would have to decide once again.

A few minutes before, there had come to ears from

the direction of the baptistery a sound—a faint scuffling. An ordinary man might not have noticed it. But since his parish had fled to the eastern half of the city, he had lived alone, in virtual silence much of the time. He even joked to himself that he could hear the lead in the remaining stained-glass windows creak as it dried out.

Now, without looking back, he knew that someone was standing at the very front of the nave.

"*Père?*" a voice came softly in strangely accented French.

"*Non,*" he answered, rising, trying to glimpse the figure through the dimness. "It is only *brother,* my friend." Suddenly he realized that a second man had entered through the back of the chancel. This one he could clearly see: a commando with blackened face in a dark fighting suit. He held a peculiar-looking automatic weapon.

The first figure was now treading down the aisle. "I am called McCoy. My friend and I need your help."

This commando held no weapons, but caution made Brother John hold his tongue.

The man halted two meters away. He tried to smile, but feelings of urgency must have stifled the expression. "We have no time to explain everything. The lives of innocent people are at stake. We believe that you have already helped us—and might help us again. If you must know, I will tell you that we are—"

"The Americans. Yes, I thought you might have reason to seek my help. What do you require?"

The one called McCoy sighed with relief. The other one grinned.

"We need some way of communicating with our people. We need a radio right away."

Brother John wished that they had asked for anything but that.

"Do you have one, Brother?"

He continued to hesitate—if only they could understand what using the radio on such short notice as this could mean. The certainty of discovery. Then the reprisals.

McCoy must have thought that he didn't have one after all, for he then asked if there was a telephone somewhere nearby.

"I am sorry . . . there has been no telephone service west of Avenue du General de Gaulle for over six months now. The company refuses to install equipment only to have it destroyed again. And many of the operators are Shia spies." Brother John folded his hands together and pressed them against his lips. "I have a radio, my friends."

"Thank you—"

"But you must understand this . . ." Sensing their great impatience, he swiftly explained the code system using the bells as well as the fear of detection by roving Syrian technicians that made this necessary. "But, my friends," he concluded, "it is the middle of the night. What can I say to Georges about the bells?"

"The Amal leader is *here?*"

"Yes, of course, next door at the garrison."

"Well, you won't have to explain to him. You're coming with us. We'll steal an auto—"

Brother John scolded the American with a wag of his forefinger. "Why break the theft commandment when God has already placed a Volkswagen at our disposal?"

The American commandos glanced at each other.

Brother John shuffled behind the altar and retrieved the radio.

As soon as he had rung the last note of the sequence that called for immediate monitoring at Phalangist headquarters, Brother John felt himself being clasped under the arms by the two Americans, who carried him in this humiliating fashion into the vestibule and then, after the one called Peterson had peeked out the front doors with ridiculous-looking eyeglasses, into the cool night itself.

"Which way, Brother?" McCoy asked.

"To the right. Follow the path through the rose garden."

Peterson kept whispering that he was sorry—a tender heart under that somewhat severe exterior.

"My friends, please let me walk for myself."

"We're sorry, Brother—honestly."

McCoy asked, "Do you think the Phalangists are monitoring yet?"

"Give them a minute more."

They lowered him into the rosebushes as two militiamen came running along the same path from the garrison toward the church.

When the Shi'ites were gone, McCoy asked, "Are you positive the message will be relayed to the Israelis?"

"If I ask . . . naturally."

"Very well, Brother—go ahead and try now."

"The exact words once again, if you please?"

McCoy carefully enunciated the meaningless syllables.

Then Brother John raised a surprised-sounding Phalangist radio operator: "Pass on without delay. Most urgent: *Tecumseh . . . go on Four, A-S-A-P . . . Little Boss.*" At McCoy's bidding, he asked the operator in East Beirut to repeat the message.

McCoy's head nodded in approval.

Then Brother John found himself being swept over the path again, the toes of his black shoes dragging the ground.

Within sight of the van, they halted and hid behind a low wall. The cobbled lane between the garrison and the church grounds was empty. McCoy whispered in his ear, "Brother, are you sure only two men are posted at the Avenue de Gaulle sentry post?

"Yes, with automatic rifles only—as I reported." He chuckled under his breath. "Amal is like a chicken. It turns its entire head each time it looks in a new direction.

This morning it expected a Christian attack from the landward side. Tonight it has everyone looking the opposite way for Israeli gunboats riding the swells."

"Very well . . . give me your keys, Brother."

"No, McCoy, I must drive. They will let me through without a second look. There are some old vestments in the back. Cover yourself with them."

The monk sat behind the wheel as the two Americans pushed the van well past the last windows of the garrison.

"Fire it up, Brother," McCoy whispered as he and Peterson leaped inside through the sliding door and quickly concealed themselves under some old chasubles and woolen *jebee* cloaks the monk had been intending to give to the poor to be used as blankets.

Suddenly two blinding headlamps swung around the curve near the vineyard. Brother John found himself so disoriented he had to brake and shield his eyes with a hand.

"What is it?" McCoy whispered.

"I don't know. A big truck, I think. We are very close to the sentry post."

Peterson was peering over the seat, his head held sideways. "Two-ton with militiamen riding the running boards. Keep moving, Brother. Please don't stop here."

One truck and then another rumbled past. Brother John flinched. Someone had screamed something at him. He hadn't understood. And he wasn't sure he could see the road. He was afraid the front wheels of the van might suddenly bounce over the berm and down into the vineyard. All at once he felt ridiculously old.

A burst of automatic weapons fire made his shoe dart to the brake pedal again. "My dear God!"

"Don't stop!" McCoy begged.

Something buzzed past Brother John's cheek. He looked back at the shattered rear window and then forward at the crazed lines radiating out from a small hole in the windshield, the glazing iridescent from the beams of several electric torches.

All at once Brother John felt confident and full of energy. That near miss had done something to him, perhaps taken him back more than forty years, awakening long-dormant instincts. "I will delay them. You two must continue."

"Brother"—Peterson had trained the submachine gun on him—"we can't let you be taken."

"You have no choice. I will not talk, my friends. In your heart you know that, yes?"

Peterson lowered his weapon.

Setting the parking brake and taking the radio off the front passenger seat, the monk stepped down from the van and began walking back toward the church. From the corner of his eye, he saw the sentries abandon their post to chase after him, waving pistols in the air, never realizing that to their backs the Americans were making use of the slight declivity along this stretch of road to coast toward Avenue du General de Gaulle.

The militiamen running toward him from the trucks did not take notice of the Volkswagen either—until it was too late and the engine coughed to life.

"Stop it! Shoot at it!" someone hollered in Arabic.

And another railed: "The old man has a radio! Seize it!"

Then the brother was knocked to the ground. His head was bleeding, and everything became so enormously confused he could not account for the time between the moment in which he was clubbed with the butt of the rifle and the point at which he was squinting through bleared eyes at Georges's face.

"Brother John . . . my old friend, what have you done to us? What have you done to our friendship?"

He tried to speak, but there was the coppery taste of blood in his mouth and his throat felt swollen half shut.

Another man stood leaning against a closed door. He held a bright, silvery pistol at his side.

"Brother John, who were the men with you?"

Think, he reminded himself, *think like the good soldier you once were.*

"Did these men give you the radio?"

The monk gasped out a weak yes.

"Phalangists?"

He did not answer—that was almost as good as saying yes. But only almost.

His face was struck by a fist, but it did not seem to come from the Amal leader's direction.

It happened again, and he realized that the man with the silver pistol was looming over him, shaking his free hand as if it stung.

"Phalangists. We can count on it, Abdul," Georges said.

"Unless our jeeps stop them."

"It is fortunate we have already taken measures to move the hostages. We must simply execute our plan with greater speed—that is all." Georges then whispered to the old man, "I am gravely disappointed. I was sure we had an understanding." Then his footfalls retreated out of the room and down a concrete corridor.

The man with the pistol—his pitiless face came into sharp focus.

The muzzle bumped against Brother John's temple. His pulse hammered against the insistent pressure. *What four very different hearts You have permitted me to glimpse this night. Peterson, who can kill, but despises it. McCoy, who can readily kill—but would never murder. Georges, who lacks the courage to do either, so he relies on the cruelty of others. And now this one, who takes pleasure from murder. But, contrary to the spirit of his vengeance, he only delivers me into Your hands, and in you I shall at last have my hermitage . . . my place in the lovely quiet of the mountains.*

23

"Here comes the cavalry!" Peterson shouted from the back of the van, reaming the rest of the glass out of the shattered rear window with a tire jack. "Two . . . no, three jeeps . . . and something bigger following them!"

"Then you don't want to see what's coming up." McCoy's night vision–equipped eyes darted from the rear-view mirror, where the approaching headlamps were squiggling like green glowworms, then back to the barricade two hundred meters in front of them. It was at least six feet high and blocked all four lanes of Avenue Ramlet el Baida. He had hoped to stay on the broad boulevard all the way out of West Beirut, keeping the sea on his right. But using this route was now out of the question. Small-arms fire was already flashing at the Volkswagen from the top of the rubble dam.

"Hang on!" He veered left sharply, almost wrapping the front bumper around a light pole on the side street he had entered.

"Goddamn you!" Peterson had been bounced around. He righted the jerry can he had been straddling and once again aimed the Israeli SMG out the window. "Take it easy!"

McCoy leaned forward, lifted the goggles off his eyes for an instant. "Jesus Christ!" He swerved to avoid a white panel truck that had suddenly turned out in front of him.

Peterson swung the SMG on the driver. In the mirror McCoy glimpsed the terrified man hoisting his arms to surrender.

"It was the newsman!" Peterson laughed. "Delivering papers to the kiosks!"

McCoy took a deep breath. "Fucking Beirut." He

was struggling to recall the map he had last studied in Israel when Peterson interrupted his concentration.

"Scott?"

"What!"

"Do you think they've killed the friar by now?"

He didn't know how to answer. Yes, he thought so, but that wasn't the thing to say right now. *Fucking Peterson.* "Look sharp—we got lights behind us again."

"Lights and muzzle flashes!" But the sergeant major held his fire. "Slow down and let me break this freaky thing in. Come on, let the bastards catch up with us!"

"Like we got a choice in this rattletrap?" McCoy fed the steering wheel through his white-knuckled hands. The gasoline in the jerry can under Peterson could be heard sloshing from side to side. "Hang on a sec . . . I got just the place." The UNESCO headquarters, which was a few blocks south of Boulevard Saeb Salaam, had given McCoy enough of a clue to where he was now to work the back streets and alleys toward the high wall surrounding the Soviet Embassy. "You still got a bandit back there?"

"Forty meters and closing!"

"Anytime, Peter!"

As Peterson opened up, McCoy smirked. *That'll get Ivan out of the sack and down on the deck with his face in his fuzzy slippers!* Now the KGB would be out the rest of the night shaking down the neighborhood for information about the crazies who'd had the balls to burst caps right outside their spy nest.

"You hit anything?" he asked Peterson.

"I don't know."

"What do you mean you don't know?"

"Well, it ain't back there anymore. But now we got another problem." Peterson chucked a couple of pieces of something over the front seat. "I just broke the gun."

"*What?*"

"You heard me."

"How?"

152

"I don't know!" the sergeant major bellowed back, sounding genuinely angry for the first time. "I finished the burst and the lower receiver group was in my lap! It's a fucking glass gun, Scott!"

McCoy turned his head to check behind. He hadn't believed what he had seen in the mirror. "One of those rigs back there is a light armored vehicle."

"Great, just great."

McCoy sped past several youthful militiamen huddling around a barrel fire in the early morning chill, too disinterested in the Volkswagen to unsling their Kalashnikovs. Without warning Peterson, he flipped a U-turn, approached the squad on his side of the van and, hanging halfway out the window, shook his fist and cried, *"Allah Akbar!"*

Reflexively, they cheered, *"Allah Akbar!"* brandishing their rifles over their heads. McCoy snatched one of the weapons out of the air by its sling and, accelerating, careened right at the next intersection.

"Do that again," Peterson said.

"It only works once." McCoy tossed him the automatic rifle.

Peterson set the jerry can back on its base. "We got Amal knocking again." With a short burst, he tried to make the lead jeep back off. "Damn . . . they don't believe me."

In a mile of zigzagging, McCoy attempted time and again to lose them—but he soon realized that the Amal drivers knew the city ten times better than he did, especially these Shia slums south of the city sports center. Skillful driving had bought him only a minute or two of lead.

Whenever headlamps appeared around a distant corner, Peterson cranked off single rounds at them, hoping to score a lucky hit on the wheel man.

"Shit! They save the best for last around here." McCoy threw the van into a panic-stop. Then he backed up into the space between two ruined buildings.

The moment before this, he had been tantalized by a view of runway lights. They were less than a kilometer now from the northern border of Beirut International. After that, it would be smooth sailing to the beach at Khalde. But between open highway and them, an armored personnel carrier was hunkered down in the middle of the road.

"Hand me some of those church clothes," he told Peterson. "And the gas can."

"What are you doing?"

McCoy spread an armful of old vestments out across the roof of the van, then doused them with gasoline. He made sure none of it trickled down near the engine in the back. "We got an M-113 APC ahead. There's room on either side to get around him."

"Good."

"But there's a troop sitting behind its .51-caliber retrofit. The secret to this is going to be *timing*. And here come Amal's defensive driving team." McCoy pulled out onto the street again and steered for the headlamps of the APC, which had now winked on.

Waving for the Amal convoy to follow as if he intended to lead it to glory, McCoy gathered speed before reaching outside and touching his butane lighter to the corner of a chasuble.

Peterson scrambled away from the rear window as it became a porthole on hell. "Scott," he asked carefully, "do you realize you just set our transportation on fire?"

McCoy ducked his head away from the roof—the thin metal was already hot. "Perfect," he muttered as he rolled up his window. From behind, the Amal vehicles continued to hard charge—and ahead a helmet popped up over the gun shields of the APC.

Peterson grasped McCoy's shoulder as the Volkswagen accelerated directly for the lights of the armored vehicle. "What the—?"

"I got a hunch about this guy."

"What if you're wrong?"

"You'll be among the first to find out. Don't worry, Peter. I used to do something like this on the highway between Escanaba and Marquette every Saturday night in summer. It's called playing chicken."

"No shit!"

With the fiery van less than one hundred meters away from him and refusing to veer from its certain collision course by a single degree, the APC gunner decided not to try to deal with fanatical martyrdom. He flew over the top of his armored shields and bellyflopped down into a ring of sandbags.

McCoy roared around the APC, then looked back through a contrail of sparks and cinders as the gunner, now humiliated into action, climbed aboard again, charged his machine gun and began peppering the Amal vehicles.

As McCoy almost went up on two wheels around a corner, a big sheet of smoldering vestments slid off the roof. Peterson crawled over the front seat, clipping McCoy in the ear with his soft shoe.

"Watch it, for Chrissake. You kicked me."

"I'll kick you," the sergeant major said ominously. "I'll kick you in the ass so godamned hard . . .!" But then he began giggling, helplessly, tearfully.

McCoy smiled at him. "Lighten up."

Nick Alexander had to ask Raffi Amir to speak louder over the rumbling of the throaty diesels of the three Israeli landing craft waiting to cast off from the dock at Haifa.

"I was wondering, Nick, if you are entirely comfortable with the message we received from Phalangist headquarters?"

"Are you trying to satisfy a personal or a professional curiosity?"

"At our age, is there a difference? We *are* our jobs."

Once again Alexander swept his eyes over the decks of all three craft. He nodded in satisfaction at the assault vehicles, the covered trucks, the motorcycles—all freshly painted with Lebanese Army markings. His thirty-three operators were rushing to stow their gear, assisted by the Israeli commandos who would man the LCs.

During the interminable day, waiting for McCoy and Peterson to infiltrate Beirut and send back word, Delta Force had rehearsed at a mock-up of the Amal brigade headquarters based on plans Mossad happened to have on file. Raffi had also located a condemned school near Atlit that approximated the interior of the Maronite facility as described by the on-ground operative in West Beirut.

Raffi was chuckling. "You did not answer me, Nick."

"Well, I guess I'm comfortable with the message—if it's authenticity you're talking about." He did not explain to the Israeli that, thanks to his Yankee mother, Tecumseh was his middle name. This, for security reasons, was known only to his operators. "I just don't want to tempt Murphy by saying I'm sure everything's just peachy on McCoy's end."

"Murphy?"

"You know—the guy with the law that says that anything that can possibly go wrong *will* go wrong."

"Ah, I know it well."

Alexander held out his hand. "I want to thank you people for all you've done—especially for the rush job on our tactical radios. We should've anticipated jamming after the Algiers operation."

Raffi shrugged. "The insidious Mr. Murphy, yes?" The thickset man clasped the colonel's hand in both of his. He started to say something, then decided to let it go. Two commandos helped him over the gunwale. He did not wait to watch the landing craft cast off and churn away from the dock.

It was just as well, Alexander thought. Raffi ought to

go home to his wife and his children. It was going to be a long war for him—perhaps for as long as he lived.

24

0300 Hours . . . The Beach at Khalde

McCoy flashed another staccato sequence from his compact, high-intensity signal lamp in the direction from which he had heard a faint grumbling of diesel engines. The stars were bright all the way down to the sea, but there was no moon—nor would there be one tonight.

He crawled up the sand dune to Peterson, who was keeping watch toward the road. "Anything?" he whispered.

"Nope." The sergeant major kept scanning the scrub through the night-vision goggles. "I think they just kept driving north."

"I'd give my eyeteeth right now to know who the hell they were."

"Well," Peterson slowly said as he turned toward the darkened village of Khalde and gave it a onceover, "they were either Shi'ite, Druze, Armenian, Palestinian or Phalangist."

"Thanks."

"Those engines sound to you like they're coming any closer?"

"I hope so." McCoy slid down the dune and signaled again from the waterline, holding the lamp close to his body. Then he sat cross-legged on the hard, moist sand.

He had just slowed the Volkswagen on the road north of Khalde, looking for a place to ditch the scorched van, when a Datsun pickup truck came flying blacked-out over the crest of a hill, its driver using only the gray luminescence of the road to guide him. Peterson was halfway out his door with the Kalashnikov when the vehicle whistled past, someone in the bed of the truck running a flashlight beam over the Volkswagen in the few seconds before the pickup was gone again over the top of another small hill.

"Dammit!" McCoy pounded the yet warm roof of the van with his fist. He had visions of Desert One—bus passengers and other assorted Iranian civilians gaping at Delta's rendezvous activities from start to finish. "Were you able to make them?"

"Militiamen of some sort. Somebody had an RPG."

McCoy had gotten behind the wheel again. "Let's run this thing down a gully someplace."

In the hour since the disconcerting appearance—and equally disconcerting disappearance—of the small pickup, the two men had seen nothing. The night grew chillier, and a slight haze was blown off by a breeze, revealing an obsidian sky flecked with stars.

After a while they had heard engines on the sea.

McCoy now came to his feet. He cupped his hand behind his ear. Then he snapped his fingers for Peterson's attention and pointed at three squat profiles due west, their wakes glowing on the water. The sergeant major replied with a hand signal that depicted masturbation.

McCoy gave the landing craft helmsmen another glimmer of beacon to head toward.

Then the first LC beached itself fifty meters north of him. Its bow ramp had no sooner slapped the shallows than the second and third craft skidded up onto the sands.

Two motorcycles churned forward across the beach. These operators were tasked with tacking down the corners of a defensive perimeter that was Delta's first priority of business.

An operator trotted past McCoy, toting an M203. "Good morning, little boss," Winnemucca said as he hurried up the dune to relieve Peterson.

"Morning, Waukene."

Finally Nick Alexander turned away from supervising the off-loading of the assault vehicles and the covered trucks. "What've we got, McCoy?"

"Pretty much what the operative passed on to the Israelis."

"How about Flight 827?"

"We've got an idea or two for taking down the plane," Peterson said. "But we'll need Winnemucca for that caper, boss."

Alexander sighed. "The 727 could prove the toughest nut to crack. But we've got to hit everything—the headquarters, the school, the plane—at the same time. Otherwise, wherever we don't hit, the bastards will kill the hostages."

"Agreed, boss," McCoy said. "We'll brief you while we're en route." He saw that most of the operators were already waiting in the trucks. "What we don't have much of is time. They're going to transport the hostages over the mountains to Bekaa anytime this morning."

"I figured as much from your message—and that's what I used on the President."

McCoy felt the old suspicion grab at his guts. "For Chrissake, we've got a *go*, don't we?"

Alexander chuckled. "To use the head honcho's exact words, 'Do it. Just do it.' " He handed new transceivers to McCoy and Peterson. "What do you say we oblige the man?"

The bags under Georges's eyes were very dark. He paced among the arguing militiamen in the brigade office. Despite his agitation, he was unable to entirely ignore it when a careless smoker dropped an ash onto the carpet he had brought from his more comfortable office downtown.

From the darkest corner of the room, Abdul watched him, took delight in his slightest movement, down to the trembling of his pale fingers.

"Fool! Fool!" Georges suddenly exploded, turning on

the bearded lieutenant who had arrived in the last hour with an absurdly small band of reinforcements from the Shia strongholds in the south. "Why did you not challenge these strange men?"

"Georges, how was I to know who they were? I was ordered to proceed directly here by *you*, was I not?"

The Amal leader counted out each verbal indictment on a finger. "You come upon two men in a Volkswagen van on a deserted stretch of the coastal road near Khalde . . . you see that they are dressed like commandos . . . even their faces are camouflaged . . . you see that they are not Lebanese . . . that one of them has fair hair . . . and yet you investigate nothing!"

"At that hour, Georges, I had no idea the van was stolen from next door by the Phalangists!"

"Not Christians, you idiot—*Americans!* Americans who . . ." All at once Georges let his voice trail off.

Hiding his smirk behind his hand, Abdul knew how to finish the man's thought for him: *Americans who spied on this very headquarters in preparation for an attack that might come any moment now!* Yet, for his own reasons Georges did not want to voice this fear—Abdul thought he knew why.

Georges coughed, then fanned the thick cigarette smoke hanging in the room away from his flushed face. "Everyone will stop smoking at once! It is not possible to breathe in here!" He clasped his hands to the side of his head. "What a terrible night! First, the American spies. Then, for absolutely no good reason, Lebanese Forces violate the cease-fire it took me months to work out, and shoot up two of our vehicles. Someone tell me why! Just tell me why!"

"I think we should now rocket two of their vehicles," a youth said, smoothing his wispy mustache with a pocket comb. "It is only fair."

"Absolutely not! It will be hard enough for me to explain why our men destroyed the APC!" Georges reached for the pack of Player cigarettes on the desk and absently lit up. "This is not the night to launch a campaign against Gemayel's mercenaries. I want our people to stay clear of them. We have enough problems—like trucks. I order the acquisition of four trucks to take the hostages to Bekaa but receive only two! I order a full brigade brought up from the south and receive six men!"

Georges stopped his frantic pacing. He took a long drag off his cigarette, then squinted through the curl of smoke at Abdul. "What are your thoughts, my brother? You are the only one around here who seems to get things done."

Abdul accepted the compliment with a nod. "I think we should begin the transfer at once."

"With only two trucks?"

"Yes. It is our best guarantee of not being attacked by the Americans. And we should phone one of the neutral embassies and tell them the hostages are already in the process of being moved to different places all over Lebanon. They will quickly pass the information on to the Americans. This will tie the U.S. President's hands."

"Excellent." Georges stood a little straighter. He turned toward one of his lieutenants: "Malik, how long before we can load up the first hostages?"

"Oh, one hour I should think. We must tie their hands together, blindfold them—"

"No, no, no!" Georges protested.

"May I make a suggestion?" Abdul asked quietly. He had already decided that he was going to salvage something for Hizbollah out of this growing chaos. He had not risked his life only to see the fruits of his bold act wither and die. A glorious reception awaited him on the other side of the mountains.

Still too infuriated to speak, Georges gestured for him to go ahead.

"Permit me to proceed immediately up the Damascus Road with the six Jews and the two Marines. The other captives will follow as transport becomes available."

Georges's eyes skipped from face to face. He scowled at the sheepish expressions he saw. "Any objections?"

No one spoke up.

"Then it is settled. Go, Abdul, with our blessings. And while you are doing that, I will personally lead a detail down to Khalde"—his eyes accused the newly arrived officer from the south—"to locate and kill the American spies who twice this night have slipped through our fingers."

Abdul smirked.

Georges's words had crept ever closer to the fact the man was trying to conceal from his brothers. An American attack was imminent, and the Amal leader had no intention of being here when it occurred.

"*Allah Akbar . . .*" Abdul slipped through the crowded room and descended two flights of stairs to the basement.

Within minutes the "special prisoners," as Georges had once referred to them, were bound at the wrists and lined up in the corridor. But before the hoods were slipped down over their dazed faces, Abdul had an inspiration. He had the guards prod them into a darkened room, the one nearest the stairs.

Then nothing more was said or done to the hostages for two minutes.

They began to fidget. *Nothing is worse than waiting for the unknown,* Abdul mused. *It is the most exquisite form of terror.*

"My friends," he finally broke the stillness, voice hushed, "we are about to go on a journey together. You may think of it as a pilgrimage. You will see new things. You will experience wondrous things. Your eyes will be opened to the truth. But you must do everything I ask you to. This time I will not threaten you. And why should I? We are good friends by now. Instead, let me show what will become of you if you disobey your Shia brothers." He flipped on a light switch.

The Roman Catholic priest moaned. The Marines simply gaped. And many of the Jews began to shiver.

"I will say no more on the matter." Abdul turned off the light. The corpse of the Maronite monk, sprawled in its own blood atop a white table, became a silhouette once again.

Rising from his chair in the gymnasium, Mustafa could not believe the news the militiaman had just brought from the nearby headquarters building. "But why does Georges need five of my men?"

The youth in a khaki shirt and faded Levi's shrugged. "They are going down to Khalde to kill the CIA spies."

"What CIA spies?"

"The two who stole the church van."

Unconsciously, Mustafa slapped the base of the curved magazine in his Kalashnikov. "But those were Phalangists." He saw several of the hostages looking up from their mattresses. "Go back to sleep—or you die!"

The youth raised a shoulder again. "I am sorry, Mustafa, but it is now being said they were Americans."

"Why am I told nothing!"

"I do not—"

"I will not be responsible for these prisoners if I am told nothing! Hours ago, with all that shooting out front, did anyone think to come and tell me what was happening? No! And do you want to see what I came close to doing?" Mustafa seized one of the prostrate hostages by the scruff of his hair and pulled him up onto his knees. Then he held the muzzle of his automatic rifle against the man's head. "I almost shot them! I almost shot every last one of them!" He hurled the American down against his mattress again.

"I am only telling you things Georges told me to say, my brother."

"Yes, yes—and you may tell Georges that I will listen no more to what he says." A thought flickered into Mustafa's mind. He said, "If the spies were indeed

163

Americans, we must be more vigilant than ever." He surveyed the fifty hostages lying on their mattresses. "Tell Abdul I have moved half of the prisoners into the classrooms. From now on, I will accept advice only from Abdul."

"But, Mustafa, he has—"

"Go!"

Alexander sat across from Bobby Lee, Winnemucca and the two other operators who were tasked with freeing the crew of Flight 827. He could not see their faces in the darkness, but he could almost feel the electricity given off by their grins. "Listen, under ordinary circumstances—if there are such things in this world—I'd never send you in this lean in the manpower department. But it gets down in numbers. We've got damn near sixty hostages at the other and only three at the airport."

"Oh, hell, boss," Bobby Lee said, "you don't need to apologize. I'd do it alone if you'd let me. One hijacking, one hillbilly—sounds fair to me."

Alexander slapped the man's shoulder. "Thanks." Then he turned toward Winnemucca, who was wiping down his .22-caliber suppressed pistol. The Paiute operator had switched clothes with one of the truck drivers, who had been loaned grungy Lebanese-motif fatigues in Haifa by Mossad. "Well, Waukene, do you feel like a Shi'ite militiaman?"

"No, sir, I feel like a woman—but we got an operation to think about."

Even McCoy, who was watching forward through a slit in the canopy, had to laugh. Then he reported, "We're being waved through another Lebanese Forces checkpoint. I can see the three-six runway lights off to our right."

"Okay," Alexander said to the four operators, "this is where we part company for a while—good luck." Rising, he joined McCoy at the look-see tear in the canvas, then rapped three times on the back of the cab to signal the driver.

"Excuse me, boss . . ." Bobby Lee said as the truck began to slow.

"Yeah?"

"Ain't you going to tell us, *hold until relieved?*"

"Bobby Lee, you've seen too many godammed war movies. I've never said that once in my entire career—even in Nam."

"*Especially* in Nam," Peterson added.

"Would you mind doing it now, Colonel?" the operator asked, his voice somber.

Alexander was glad his simper was concealed by darkness. "All right, Staff Sergeant Robert Edwin Lee—I'm ordering you to hold until relieved."

Bobby Lee's voice welled up out of the brief silence: "Shee-it! This is for real, ain't it!"

25

0443 Hours . . . Beirut

Lying on his back in a trickle of what he hoped was more water than sewage, McCoy wormed the fiber-optic probe up through the butterfly valve he had just broken open with his knife. Then he pressed his eyes against the rubber grommet in the closed-circuit module at his end of the hard-wire. The tiny lens was still a few inches below the rusted drain plate. Gently, he jiggled the flexible line and eased it upward.

At last he had a full but rounded view of the corridor in the basement of the Amal brigade headquarters.

"This is it," he whispered to the operator directly behind him in the thirty-inch-diameter sewer line. The man handed him the charge.

McCoy worked quickly. First light had been a faint but noticeable aura behind the Shouf Mountains as he and the three operators on his entry team had infiltrated toward the mouth of the sewer pipe. Now he only hoped the old adage that it was always darkest before the dawn was true, and that this would help Delta as it closed a perimeter around the headquarters and the church complex.

Before ducking into the pipe, he had seen through his night-vision equipment where Peterson's section had already crept up to the school building and was preparing to scale it. Amal did not have much manpower outside—which was good and bad. Good in the sense that it made it easier for Delta to set up. Bad in that Shia firepower would be concentrated inside the structures to start slaying hostages when the big moment arrived.

Now, with the plastic explosives charge in place, McCoy inspected his work with the small flashlight he held in his mouth. Satisfied, he consulted his watch, then set the timer. He signaled for everyone to squirm backward all the way to the elbow in the line which was closed off with a rusted gate valve. The rearguard operator had been working the last several minutes to open this obstruction—and now succeeded. The effluent that flowed out of that long-closed concrete pipe made McCoy bury his face in his jump-suit sleeve, but he fell in behind the others as they wriggled inside the branch off the main.

The valve was forced shut again. The operators put their hands over their ears and opened their mouths.

McCoy counted the seconds.

Alexander had decided that Delta was already too shorthanded for him to establish a command post outside the immediate thick of things. Nor had he remained at the assembly area. He had infiltrated with the element that would silence the antiaircraft gun's quartet of 23mm cannon and the antitank gun in the bunker, then enfilade any Amal reinforcements that might try to come up the narrow lane from Avenue du General de Gaulle. The sentry post on that lane no longer existed. It guards were now lying in the vineyard with red grins on their throats.

Glancing up, the colonel compared the paling of the sky against the sprays of black needles on the pine overhead. Another twenty minutes and it would be bright enough to distinguish colors. He ached to get going. But his watch demanded another four minutes of his patience.

The operator beside him had gone prone with the M203 he had borrowed from Winnemucca, ready to dump a high explosive round on the Soviet-built gun. Another operator, farther along the line of trees between the vineyard and the school soccer field, had turned away from his HK21 machine gun and was shouldering a LAW, a 66mm rocket with a one-time, disposable launcher tube. This particular round would deliver a shaped charge against the outer bunker wall, one that would burn through the concrete, then erupt into a murderous explosion on the other side.

He thought of his operators at the airport. By now they would have slipped through the loose Lebanese Forces cordon, crossed the darkened north-sound runway and would be closing on the 727. Momentarily, Winnemucca would peer right through the metal skin of the fuselage with an infrared camera, determining the locations of all warm bodies within the craft. Then he would make his approach alone—the loneliest job in the world, for the few minutes it lasted.

Alexander folded back his sleeve to see his watch.

"Get ready," he said to the operator with the grenade launcher.

Then, lightly, he tapped the man's shoulder.

*   *   *

As Winnemucca sauntered across the darkened tarmac toward Flight 827, he waited for the distant blasts to reverberate across the sleeping city.

He didn't think they would be heard inside the aircraft. The auxiliary power unit was softly humming, although at last report it had been shut down by order of the terrorists because they imagined it to be a trick by the crew to waste fuel. Perhaps, when the on-board batteries had gone low, they'd seen for themselves the necessity in keeping the APU purring.

The militiamen had insisted that no airport floodlights be directed on the 727, but that the Lebanese Forces soldiers lounging around the terminal building be brightly illuminated. The result was a huge lake of shadow around Flight 827, which the four operators had swiftly trotted across.

They had halted a hundred meters out, and Winnemucca had taken a look at the fuselage through the infrared equipment. The human shapes in the cabins were distinct, but those in the cockpit were a fused, glowing mass. He couldn't tell how many individuals were there—at least three, he had thought.

Once again he had run through the entire operation with mental flash cards. He would forget nothing, even down to the dead terrorists being stored in the forward cargo hold for later identification.

But now it was time to do it. The other operators ran into the darkness, and Winnemucca slowly walked toward the rear of the aircraft.

The tail section loomed overhead, but he didn't vary his easy, almost careless stride. Ahead he had a vague impression that Bobby Lee and the other two operators were already in place, squatting under the belly of the plane.

It was time to be like the Coyote, the trickster who could turn himself into many different beings. The Coyote was not a raven, but he could make himself look as if he were flying. He was not a man, but he could make himself look as if he were walking upright.

In truth, Winnemucca spoke but a handful of Arabic words, and most of them were not appropriate for this occasion. But he would now make himself look as if he had always been a Shi'ite.

It was a matter of confidence. The Coyote, for all his faults, had enormous confidence.

Winnemucca grinned in a way he had never grinned before. His eyes glistened with a new and strange aspect.

A flashlight beam swept down from the window of the port rear service door. It blinded him, but he shouted, *"Allah Akbar!"* as he held up a folded piece of blank paper as if it were a message.

The beam continued to shine, but around its brilliance he could espy two faces in the window—both of them with suspicious-looking eyes.

Become the Coyote.

"Allah Akbar!"

Then, as he knew it would, the ventral airstairs began to descend.

One way or another, the Coyote always got his way.

26

0439 Hours

The pall of smoke and concrete dust had not cleared out of the corridor when McCoy burst up through the jagged hole. His light-enhancing goggles trained on the stairs at the end of the passageway, he reached behind to help the next operator out of the breach in the floor.

Then, as soon as the rest of the team was crouched behind him, McCoy and the first operator rushed through an open door at precisely the same instant, vacating the rectangular opening and flattening themselves against the inside walls as swiftly as possible.

Dividing the interior space between them, they swung their Heckler & Koch 9mm "room cleaners" in alignment with the sweep of their gazes. Nothing. McCoy shouted, "Clear!" and then they covered the other two operators as the men leapfrogged ahead to find out what lay beyond the next threshold.

Two bolted steel doors were blown off their hinges with small charges.

Finding neither terrorists nor hostages thus far, McCoy was preparing to exit the next to last room when an SMG burped twice in the corridor. He came out low.

A militiaman was lying in a twisted heap at the foot of the stairs, his glazed eyes turned upward, as if he were trying to inspect the two holes in his forehead.

Not waiting to be congratulated, the operator who'd done the shooting joined his partner in a rush for the only remaining uncleared room in the basement. Silently, McCoy invited more militiamen to come stumbling down the stairs.

"Little boss!"—a forced whisper.

McCoy backed inside the room, covering the flight of stairs until the man behind him had a clear shot at the next landing. Only then did he turn around.

"Shit." It was Brother John. Half of his skull was in a dozen or more shards on the floor. They crackled underfoot as the operators moved to check a storage closet.

"Jesus, do you think they've already snuffed everybody?"

"No—this was our inside man," McCoy said.

"Then I don't get it. Where are our people? What about the mattresses in these rooms, little boss?"

"It smells like sweat down here. I'd say they've been moved in the last hour."

"Upstairs?"

"Let's find out."

Peterson leaned far out over the edge of the gymnasium building. A rope looped once through a carabiner attached to his body harness kept him from tumbling forty feet below. A CAR-15 assault rifle was slung across his chest. His face was covered by a protective polycarbonate mask, his hands by gloves—although the material covering his trigger finger had been cut away.

He could look down between his legs and see lighted windows. The glazing of the lower ones was reinforced with chicken wire, but the upper panes were made of ordinary glass.

In seconds things would start blowing up all around him: the antiaircraft gun, the bunker, Amal's motor pool parked outside the old garrison building. A fourth explosion would breach the stone wall on the east side of the church complex, and—when not raking militiamen with M60 machine-gun fire—Delta's two assault vehicles would begin mowing down the pipes that could prevent the Sixth Fleet Sea Stallion helicopters from landing on the soccer field. As all of this was happening, an operator on the ground below Peterson would smash out a small window and toss a silent ignition flash-bang grenade inside the gym.

But the sergeant major put these things out of his mind. Instead, he worked on galvanizing his energies and concentration with jolts of adrenaline. He fixated on the precise things he must do his first seconds inside the gymnasium. He, like every other operator, had logged hundreds of hours inside the House of Horrors, the special shooting facility at the Stockade. There, firing away at sophisticated motion-picture projections of terrorist-hostage situations, he had become too cagey for the simulations to trick him into a bum shot. He had always bagged the bad guys—and never even scratched the good guys.

But *that* had been a movie.

Across the roof, a second operator was hanging off another polyester rope, waiting to sail through the windows on the opposite side of the building.

Peterson gave him a thumbs-up. It was quickly returned.

Then somebody lit off a LAWS rocket, and Peterson leaped out into space. His shoes touched bricks only once before he pushed away from the wall again. Then he came crashing through the windows, his face turned aside and his chin tucked down. The last flash of a stun-grenade sequence of five was winking out as he tumbled against the hardwood floor, striking it with his hip and then his left shoulder. But before these places had begun to hurt he was on his feet, swinging his CAR-15 around without delaying to unsling it. "Americans—stay down!" he heard his own voice cry. *Plink-plink. Plink-plink.* He swiveled his muzzle toward the other militamen he had glimpsed, but the second operator had already dropped them.

Without pausing to admire his handiwork, Peterson raced to secure one of two corridors connecting the gym to the adjacent classrooms.

For a split second he had wondered if it had only been the movie inside the House of Horrors.

Still suspicious of the militiamen he had never seen before, the Shi'ite descended the airstairs only two steps before reaching out his hand for the message. His Kalashnikov was trained on Winnemucca's abdomen. Voice insistent, he asked the operator a question in Arabic.

Winnemucca told him he was an idiot—in Paiute.

Bewildered, the man turned his head no more than two inches as if to summon someone from the front cabin. His upper body twisted slightly in the same direction. But more importantly, the muzzle of the rifle canted downward and to the right.

That was all Winnemucca needed. In the same instant he leaned to the left, the operator drew the .22-caliber silencer-equipped pistol out of his shoulder harness and put two divots in the militiaman's head: one in the temple and one behind the ear.

The man crumpled over and tobogganed down the airstairs on his face. Winnemucca ran over the top of him into the tourist cabin, firing down the length of the aisle at another terrorist and hitting him twice in the chest. A third militiaman, hearing the body collapse against the deck, reared up from his makeshift bed of three adjoining seats. He reached for his Kalashnikov only after he had locked gazes with the operator, smiled in greeting—then realized the gravity of his blunder.

Winnemucca would have felled him but for Bobby Lee's entry through the starboard wing escape hatch, which the operator had jimmied rather than blown. Both of his whispering rounds scored on the back of the terrorist's head. He was followed inside by an operator who immediately crept forward to attach a stethoscope to the cockpit door, which was closed, and plug up the peephole with his wad of chewing gum.

The fourth Delta man had come bounding up the airstairs two seconds behind Winnemucca. Having made sure that no one was hiding in the lavatories, he was now going through the overhead hand luggage compartments —they wanted no ugly surprises to pop up behind their backs.

The operator at the cockpit door signaled that he could hear nothing inside.

Using the top of his foot, Bobby Lee rolled over the body that was bleeding onto the aisle carpeting of the first-class cabin. Winnemucca's long shots had punched two holes in the man's sternum, but Bobby still checked for a neck pulse. Then, catching Winnemucca's eye, he pointed meaningfully at the slack-jawed face.

Waukene nodded that he had already made the identification. It was Jaffar Ibn Khalil, the only one of the three original hijackers Delta knew by name and mug shot, thanks to his arrest at Athens Airport.

Grinning, Bobby Lee licked his forefinger and drew a big X in the air over Jaffar's face.

Winnemucca clenched a fist, then clicked his eyes toward the cockpit. Bobby and the other operator nodded in agreement.

Lee tested the latch a fraction of an inch; it wasn't locked.

Using his fingers, not his voice, Waukene counted out one . . . two . . . and then the three men charged inside the cockpit and startled the crew awake.

The pilot bolted upright in his seat, afraid to turn around, trying to identify the intruders by their reflections in the windscreen glass. The co-pilot had come to his feet, as had the flight engineer, who was backed up against his instrument console—both men unable to take their eyes off Winnemucca's sepia complexion.

At last the pilot turned, his face haggard looking, his eyelids sleep swollen. "Who are you?"

Bobby Lee shrugged, then drawled, "Well, it looks like I'm your prince in shining armor, Sleeping Beauty."

"What are you doing here?"

"I guess we come to kiss your ass awake. Nightmare's over, Captain Campbell." The staff sergeant offered his hand. "Welcome back to the world."

27

0446 Hours

Dawn.

McCoy crouched at the front doors to the Amal brigade headquarters, peering across a jumble of scorched vehicles and through the wan first light of day at Mr. Lebanon Maronite School.

The HK21 machine gun was bickering with a sniper. All at once the sniper stopped talking back.

McCoy glanced over his shoulder. Nine men were crouched behind him. Seven were from his section: the two entry teams that had just cleared the building from top and bottom at the same time.

Two of the men were wearing flex-cuffs. They, unlike nine of their compatriots laid out cold in the corridors and rooms of the headquarters, had chosen life over martyrdom. On their foreheads were the letters *IE,* drawn with an indelible highlighter, marking them for immediate extradition. Tonight they would sleep aboard the carrier *Nimitz*— and then it was on to a United States federal detention facility.

"Okay, let's go lend a hand next door."

Six of the operators jogged behind him across the narrow lane to the Maronite complex. One man split off with the prisoners, herding them toward the soccer-field landing zone.

A familiar wop-wop-wop sound made McCoy look out across the Mediterranean. Five Sea Stallion helicopters were hugging the waves as they headed for Beirut International. There they would off-load a company of Sixth Fleet Marines, who would secure the area around Flight 827 and keep the north-south runway open and

175

unobstructed. Then the choppers would begin shuttling freed hostages to the airport.

Above this activity, yet unseen, was an aircap of fighter aircraft. And in minutes, if not already, two AC-130 Spectre gunships would be on station, one above the runway and one above where McCoy now trotted—each capable of chewing a small army to pieces in seconds with its array of guns and sophisticated target-finding equipment.

McCoy found Alexander inside the gymnasium, talking into his transceiver mike. With a wave of his hand, he told the major to stand by.

The hostages were waiting in a long line, huddled against the wall. McCoy took a quick head count: forty-six. They looked relieved. Nevertheless, there was still too much gunplay going on for them to start celebrating.

"All right, Scottie . . ." Alexander finally turned to him. "That was our Israeli friends. They've just pulled out."

McCoy recalled that the landing craft had remained on the beach near Khalde only as a safety valve in case Delta Force had run into overwhelming resistance before it could penetrate West Beirut. In actuality, the convoy had encountered fewer problems getting into the city than Peterson and he had had in getting out last night.

"And the commandos say a string of jeeps and armored vehicles is smoking their way," Alexander went on. "It's flying a green Amal flag."

"Air strike?" McCoy asked hopefully.

The colonel shook his head no. "Vengeance is low on my priority list right now." But then he smirked. "Besides, the Israelis say they're leaving a surprise for them."

Then both men winced as a grenade went off somewhere in the building.

"Shit," Alexander said. "Pete's section is working the east wing of classrooms. How about helping out on the west side?"

"On our way." McCoy waved for his section to follow. Through a smashed-out window, he glimpsed a Sea Stallion banking down toward the soccer field. Behind it, an F-14 streaked across the dim, purplish sky—laying down a sonic boom to let all of Beirut know the Navy was in town.

With Delta's manpower now largely concentrated inside the school, McCoy could fall back on standard four-man rushes of rooms. They leapfrogged ahead of a three-man team already working the corridor, dropping off an operator to bring that unit up to snuff. But before they could charge through the door, McCoy's point man halted them, hand signaling that he had heard someone inside the room, probably brushing against the lath and plaster wall, McCoy surmised.

Taking a small convex auto mirror from his top jump-suit pocket, the operator inched it inside the door at its very bottom, then cried, "Midwall!"

McCoy drilled right through the plaster with a burst from his SMG.

Taking no chances, the team rushed the room and gave the sprawling militiamen two more rounds—both to the head.

The next door was locked.

One of the operators, in addition to his .45 pistol, carried a SPAS 12 shotgun on a sling. He now came forward, took aim and blew the hinges off the door with two rounds of rifled slug.

Inside that room was a scene straight out of the House of Horrors.

The four kneeling figures, all dressed in militia khaki, turned their faces toward the Delta team as it flowed across the varnished surface of the toppled door, but there was something pathetic about their expressions, their befuddled eyes that made McCoy hesitate and swing his SMG in the other direction—toward a pile of mattresses from which the barrel of a Scorpion submachine gun now extended. McCoy, reeling, loosed a burst, but not before the Scorpion's mouth flashed once, twice. He felt himself being hurled back, thrown against the wall, which he slowly slid down as he ripped off a longer burst that chopped up the mattresses.

Fighting for each breath, McCoy looked down at the front of his jump suit. There were two small holes in the Gore-Tex.

"Medic!" one of the operators shouted down the corridor toward the gymnasium.

McCoy, regaining his breath, chuckled. "It's okay."

One of the hostages had risen and was pointing at the body the operators had just dragged out of the pile of mattresses. "The bastard made us get in these clothes!" Tears welled up in the man's eyes. "His name is Mustafa. He was on the plane from the start!"

Doctor Jack came skidding through the door. He took one look at the placement of the holes, then grinned.

"Just knocked the wind out," McCoy said. "Give me a sec . . ."

The medic unzipped the front of McCoy's jump suit and brushed the two flattened bullets off his Kevlar vest. "So anyways, I still want to look you over when things quiet down."

"I'm fine, and we've still got eight people to account for." McCoy came to his feet with the medic's help, who then picked the major's SMG up off the floor for him. At that instant McCoy saw through the shattered windows of the classroom a militiaman charging against the HK21 machine-gun position, screaming and waving his Kalashnikov. The Delta gunner must have been caught in the middle of reloading, for he didn't answer the one-man banzai attack. McCoy was reaching for his SMG when Doctor Jack used it to drop the Shi'ite with a three-shot burst.

"Damn," he said, "that's twice this morning I've had to violate my Hippocratic oath."

Then Doctor Jack's hands began to shake. They always trembled after he shot someone, but this never stopped him from doing it the next time he had to. It was just his personal chemistry. McCoy clapped him around the shoulders. "When this is over, I'm going to pay your way through medical school."

"Why? I've already forgotten twice as much as they'll ever know."

"Little boss?" An operator stood in the doorway.

"Yo!"

"See the colonel on the double."

Alexander and Peterson were crouched around a militiaman whose nose was bloodied and his right eye already puffing up. The sergeant major was grilling him in Arabic. Sniveling now, the man mentioned something about Bekaa, but he was talking too fast for McCoy to understand much.

"We got a line on eight of our hostages," Alexander said out of the corner of his mouth. "This guy's a lieutenant from a unit that just came up from the south. Some joker named Abdul—sound familiar?—allegedly took the two Marines and the six Americans with Jewish-sounding names away in a truck with an escort of two armored vehicles."

"To Bekaa?"

"Sounds that way."

Peterson held his hand for the lieutenant to shut up —the man was begging for humanitarian treatment. "Okay," the sergeant major said, "they departed just before we hit. He's positive they would've gone via the Damascus Road."

"What do you say, boss?" McCoy asked. "Do we take everybody home this trip?"

Alexander exhaled, then touched a hand to his headset as some traffic came over his transceiver. "Delta copies," he said after a moment. "Fucking great—the C-141 transport developed hydraulic problems. It's turning back toward Egypt."

"What's new?" McCoy then lowered his voice. "Nick, please, can we go after our people?"

Alexander fretted over his watch for a few seconds. "Shit, take the goddamned motorcycles and try to catch them. I'll have one of the Sea Stallions stand by to pick you up on the road after you effect the rescue. But—" He made sure McCoy and Peterson were looking him straight in the eye. "Under no circumstances are you to go down into the Bekaa Valley. You are not to take it upon yourselves to start the Third World War. Do you hear me?"

Grinning, McCoy shrugged. "Got it."

"Now," Alexander continued, "if that 727 is still in good shape, I'll have it fly the first load of hostages out. That means the last train out of Beirut will be our own Hercules—in one hour. Do you hear me?"

Georges lay across the dewy sands, squinting through his binoculars at what appeared to be a foxhole and the crown of an Israeli-style helmet. He was waiting for one of his people to return from a reconnaissance on the suspicious diggings at the base of a dune near the waterline. It had been fifteen minutes now, and in that time the light had grown strong enough for a man to read the words of the Koran—the gauge by which one could tell if day had completely dawned.

The sand everywhere was dimpled with bootprints and streaked with tire tracks—trucks, armored vehicles perhaps, even motorcycles. A joint American-Zionist expedition had definitely landed here during the night, then left a man behind to guard the beach while it made mischief in West Beirut. The evidence of this mischief was the explosions Georges had been hearing for the last ten minutes.

Surely, the hostages would now either be rescued or slain. The middle path, which Georges had earnestly sought, was no longer open. But he himself would survive to rail against this act of superpower terrorism perpetrated by the U.S. President—whichever course this morning's events took. Perhaps he would even make a speech at the United Nations. He smiled at the mental image: the General Assembly rising to its feet, cheering.

At last his man had returned.

"Well, what is it?"

The militiaman took a moment to catch his breath. "Definitely . . . there is someone hiding there. I can hear a radio inside the hole. And I'm sure the helmet moved."

"Good . . . good." Georges gave the signal, and a mortar made a loud *thunk!* five meters behind him.

The first round made a geyser seethe up out of the surf. But the second attempt, to everyone's satisfaction, landed squarely on the Israeli soldier.

Now it was time for Georges to be visible to his men. It must be repeated later in West Beirut that he, of thirty Amal militiamen, was the first to rush the Israeli machine-gun nest.

"Stay back," he shouted over his shoulder. Then, thrusting one hand in a pocket of his slacks and clutching his pistol with the other, he ambled toward the position.

There was not much left in the enlarged hole—nothing of the body to be seen. But he thought he recognized the shattered remnants of an old-style field radio.

Then it caught his eye: a camouflage-green map case resting half opened on the slope of a nearby dune. Perhaps the Americans had mislaid the entire plan to their operation—what damning evidence that would be in the hands of the World Court. More foolish mistakes had been made by men in war, Georges mused as he walked toward it.

Suddenly he halted. It had felt as if something had snagged the cuff of his slacks. He glanced down at the monofilament fishing line he had tripped. Then, screaming, he turned to run—but a great force like a swarm of iron bees buzzing around his ears picked him up and drove him forward over delicate tracings of sea foam that quickly faded before his eyes.

28

0535 Hours

Captain Campbell stood at the cockpit door watching them stream up the airstairs and into the aft cabin, men he had never expected to see again, their faces scraggly with several days' growth. How many days? He tried to remember but quickly gave up. It didn't really matter—it was almost over.

There was a bloodstain in the first-class cabin aisle. He asked himself how he felt about that. But the only answer he came up with was relief that it wasn't from another one of his passengers, or from one of his crew members. And to be perfectly honest, he was glad it wasn't his.

Ten minutes before, Sergeant Lee had asked him, "Sir, do you think this bird can still fly a hundred miles?"

"You bet—the bastards topped off the tanks every twelve hours. Where to?"

"Haifa, Israel." Except that the sergeant pronounced it *Hayfuh.*

"Just give me the word."

"Well, it'll be a few minutes before the other folks are brought across town in the choppers. As usual, we got ourselves a transportation problem. The Sea Stallions got to take the Marines out, and a C-141 we had coming, ain't."

"That's fine with me. I prefer to take my ship out with me."

"What happens if you couldn't?"

"Sergeant?"

"I mean, would they dock your pay or something?"

"No . . . at least I don't think so."

Now, gently shutting the cockpit door, Campbell took his seat and, on a whim, cracked his side window so he could listen to the whistling of the turbofans. It was the sweetest sound in the world.

Someone knocked on the door. The three crewmen stiffened, then smiled at each other as Sergeant Lee stuck his head inside the cockpit. "Pardon me, gentlemen, but I want to make sure you hold on a few minutes before taking off."

"We're still awaiting your word, Sergeant. Is there a problem?"

"Oh, the grunts report some infiltrators at the end of the runway. So a gunship's going to make a little flyby."

Then, through the windscreen, Campbell watched as an AC-130 banked against the gray-green foothills of the Shouf Mountains. Suddenly, what Campbell approximated to be five acres of scrub at the south end of runway three-six seemed to levitate about twenty feet, then vaporize into smoke.

Dave Hoskins, the flight engineer, returning from having secured the airstairs, looked out and gasped, "Jesus —what was that?"

"Oh, well, sir, we had ourselves some unauthorized folks at the end of the runway," Sergeant Lee said, trying to wipe the camouflage paint off his face with a paper towel from one of the lavatories. "Staff Sergeant Winnemucca and I have been ordered to remain with you all, sir, even on the ground in Israel."

"Sergeant, you guys can ride my airplane anytime you want."

"Why, thank you, sir. Thank you very much." Lee considered the pilot's offhand remark for a moment, then looked as if he wanted to ask for something before finally thinking better of it.

When the sergeant began to shut the door, Campbell said, "Go ahead and leave it open. You can't imagine what it's like to hear people laughing back there again."

Within minutes they were in the air. For Campbell it felt like the first time he had ever flown. Once again, after all these years, the dulling effects of routine, it was pure freedom.

Leaning halfway out of his co-pilot's chair, Jim Montgomery looked aftward and chuckled. "Staff Sergeant Winnemucca just broke into the liquor—he's passing around the miniatures like they're cigars."

"Good for him." Campbell smiled at Montgomery, then turned to Hoskins. His face became serious. "I want to thank both you guys. I could've never made it without your help. I've had the best damned crew I could ever want."

All at once the strains of "The Battle Hymn of the Republic" were coming through the open door. Montgomery joined in with his rich baritone for a verse or two, but then he was overcome. He turned his face toward his side window, his shoulders shaking slightly.

When it was over, Sergeant Lee could be heard saying, "Well, damn what if that wasn't real pretty—but how about giving equal time to 'Dixie' now?"

There were several jocular boos from the tourist cabin, where all the formers hostages had sat together, without an empty seat among them.

"What'd you all say?" Lee asked, his voice feigning dismay.

The boos were repeated.

"Well, hell's bells, that's the kind of attitude what got you people in trouble in the first place."

* * *

The warm sunlight was working like a narcotic on McCoy.

Peterson and he were flashing in and out of the cool shadows of evergreen oaks along the twisting mountain road. The sudden blazes of sun made him want to pull over and just lie down in the soft dust of the shoulder. The sergeant major looked as drowsy as McCoy felt. He was leaning against the handlebars, blinking repeatedly whenever the bright, flat rays hit him full in the face.

They had talked one of the Sea Stallion pilots into airlifting their motorcycles and them south of the city to where Rue de Damas became the highway to Damascus. They'd asked the same Marine captain to pass the word along to everybody working the skies this morning: steer clear of the mountain road. McCoy was afraid one thunderous flyby of an F-14 might be enough to spook Colonel Abdul into killing his hostages.

Seven miles outside Beirut, the operators had come upon their first roadblock—a light machine gun set up at the edge of a Druze village. A few tracer rounds were lofted over their heads.

Shouting against the wind, Peterson suggested that they rocket it with one of the 66mm multishot launchers attached to the bikes. But McCoy shook his head no. He didn't want to find the Druze position ten times as strong if, by some foulup, they had to make the return trip with the hostages by road. So they veered the knobbly tired motorcycles off the pavement and crashed through the woodlands for a quarter mile, rejoining the highway well beyond the village.

Now McCoy raised up off the seat and peered forward. He had just caught a scintillation off a vehicle window on a curve two or three miles ahead. A moment later a covered two-ton truck could be seen rounding a distant bend.

Peterson was grinning. He too had glimpsed it.

McCoy pantomimed drawing a cavalry saber and

pointing it forward; the sergeant major brought a bugle to his lips.

The adrenaline boost had come at the right moment. McCoy began feeling much better. It was a good mountain road for bikes. They sped through a stand of rangy pines —the pitchy smell was delicious.

Emerging from the trees, they crested a rise on the fly and landed with a light armored vehicle squatting in the middle of the road a hundred meters ahead of them. The green Amal flag was fluttering off the radio antenna.

"Shit!" McCoy said down his bike and skidded into the scrub just as the machine gun opened up. He lay perfectly still in a choking cloud of dust, trying to decide how badly hurt he was. The Gore-Tex of his jump suit was torn away from his leg. Yet, wiping away the blood with his sleeve, he decided he'd suffered nothing more serious than the makings of a huge strawberry scab on his calf. "Peter!" he shouted over the barking of what sounded like a .51-caliber gun.

"Yo!" Wisps of dust were rising from the brush on the opposite side of the road.

"You okay?"

"Yeah—but I'm taking it real slow. A rocket pack got smashed up. I don't want a candle to cook off."

McCoy realized then that one of his own launchers had been sheared off by the fall. But the other tube assembly was still in one piece, and he quickly detached it.

Listening to bullets snip branches over his head, McCoy crawled forward until he found a sparse place in the brush that opened onto a view of the vehicle, whose militiamen had now decided to punch holes in the woodlands with a recoilles rifle.

McCoy swung the boxlike rocket launcher up onto his right shoulder and clasped the oversized trigger with both hands.

The armored vehicle disappeared under a gorgeous incendiary splash. "Peter, let's go!"

Within seconds they were roaring around the burning hulk, continuing up the road at full throttle.

"We've got to find us something like an S-curve!" McCoy shouted, keeping an eye out for the small Amal convoy, which he expected to come into view again any moment. "Or some high ground so we can take out the other armored vehicle!"

Peterson nodded. "You climb when we do! I'll come in from behind and below!"

The opportunity came a mile later when McCoy saw the apron to a dirt road that branched off from the macadam. He could see where this trace paralleled the main highway—but also kept well above it. He waved good-bye to Peterson and crouched as the lane snaked through a tunnel of sedges, across a marshy creek, and finally cut along the face of a steep slope. From here McCoy could see the covered truck, perhaps two hundred meters below. A militiaman was manning the tailgate with a Kalashnikov, one of the canvas flaps tied back so he could fire on any pursuers.

Scanning forward along the ribbon of pavement, McCoy saw the second armored vehicle. It had pulled ahead of the slower truck. And now closing within a quarter mile of the convoy was Peterson, flopped over the handlebars to lessen his wind resistance.

Hoping that the sergeant major would receive his thoughts, McCoy silently begged Peterson to find some way to take out the militiaman in the back of the truck—without being cut down himself.

Over the next five minutes, McCoy also flattened himself against the wind and streaked at more than sixty miles an hour along the dirt road, nearly colliding with a wood hauler and his donkey on one blind curve. At last he was directly above the Amal convoy.

Then it was laid out below him: a steep grade for which the road nearly twisted back in on itself. *This has to be done fast or not at all.* Braking hard, then dumping the bike on its side, McCoy ripped off the launcher again. He went prone and waited a few breathless seconds for the light armored vehicle to creep into his sights.

He squeezed off a rocket.

A miss. Instantly, it set a wide circle of scrub a blaze.

A quick glance told him that Peterson was bearing down on the truck. The Kalashnikov opened up.

Exhaling, then slowly taking a breath, McCoy fired again at the armored vehicle. It sprouted sparking garlands of fire, then became an orange fireball as its gasoline tank blew.

Throwing aside the launcher, McCoy climbed on the bike and careened back and forth down the mountainside. But then he spilled over on a patch of scree, and the engine died. Instead of restarting it, he retrieved his SMG and continued on foot, bounding down the slope as if he were skiing moguls.

There was more small-arms fire below. Then, as suddenly as it had started, the clatter stopped. There was something dire, ugly about the silence that followed.

McCoy bounded down off the slope onto the road so hard he hit the macadam on his knees and one hand.

The truck was stopped dead in the road. One militiaman had tumbled out the back, his Kalashnikov beside him but not in his grasp. A rivulet of blood trickled out of his coat sleeve and wended its way across the pavement toward the far berm. A second man was jammed in the space between the open driver's door and the cab, his foot twisted back underneath him and a pistol on the macadam three feet directly below his slack hand. The wheel man had taken a round to the chest and the face.

Good work, Peter.

But the sergeant major was nowhere to be seen.

The passenger-side door was wide open—like it had been thrown back by someone in a hurry to exit the vehicle.

Burning leaves. McCoy, in a fleeting instant, was

reminded of Michigan in autumn. His errant rocket had set the woods aflame, and pungent smoke was now sifting his way. He then realized that he could hear the crackling of dry branches being consumed by fire. Peterson's motorcycle was no longer running, drowning out all softer noises.

Quietly, McCoy approached the back of the truck. He could hear movement inside the bed. One canvas flap had already been tied back. He swung his SMG over the tailgate—right into the terror-stricken face of a Roman Catholic priest. There were six hostages behind him, all in the same state of dumb shock. Instead of crying out in relief, they only stared back at McCoy. Then one of them, an old man in a filthy shirt that had once been white, pointed toward the downward slope.

McCoy nodded that he understood. He handed a young man with a military haircut his .45 pistol and signaled for everyone to remain in the truck.

One hostage was missing, as was the militiaman who had sat in the shotgun seat of the cab.

The smoke now paled the sun, turned it the color of quicksilver.

McCoy went prone and crawled up to the lip of the berm. Over the barrel of his SMG, he looked down on a grassy mountainside.

Ed Jones had waited for this moment during the eternity that had been the last week. But now that it had arrived, he felt close to vomiting. Still, he looked for an opportunity to bowl the Iranian over the tailgate and onto the gray blur of pavement below. But the man must have been reading his mind, for he suddenly pivoted on his knees and warned the hostages with the point of his Kalashnikov.

"We got nothing in mind," Jones said to him. "We're cool. You just do your job and we'll do ours." He kept distracting the Iranian with chatter because a motorcycle had just rounded the wooded bend behind them and was closing fast.

The Revolutionary Guard heard the approaching engine. He opened fire.

Then, as he watched the motorcycle rider hoist a car-15 over the handlebars, Jones screamed, "Down—everybody down!"

The driver of the truck was braking with everything he had. The squeal was piercing.

Staring into his own lap, his lips busy with a prayer, Jones heard the CAR-15 open fire in a burst that swept completely past the truck before it ended.

The militiaman was no longer squatting in the back of the bed. He had fallen outside—unfortunately, taking his Kalashnikov with him. Jones met the gazes of the other hostages. They were looking to him to do something. The truck had come to a complete stop, and it was time for him to do something.

Trying desperately not to rock the truck, he crept toward the tailgate, balancing himself on his tethered hands as he eased toward the opening, keeping to the side on which the flap was still down.

Then a silver pistol slid past his eyes, muzzle aimed at the other hostages. In the same instant that there was a loud report inches from his ears, the Marine leaped for Abdul's arm, forcing it down.

"You die first!" Abdul shouted.

Jones flew out the back of the truck, wrapping himself around the man's trunk and pressing him to the ground. Once on the macadam, his head buzzing from having struck the surface, Jones fumbled for the Kalashnikov with his joined hands—but Abdul stopped him by touching the cold steel of the Beretta to his forehead.

I'm going to die, and there's not a thing I can do about it. It was the resignation in his inner voice that filled Jones with enormous sadness. In the distance, worlds away, someone was crashing down off the hillside through the brush. *Has to be someone from Delta Force. What will this trooper see when he finally gets down here?* The answer seemed overwhelmingly obvious. Jones struggled not to sob; he felt as if he were a child about to be unfairly punished.

But then he glimpsed something in Abdul's eyes: hesitation. Ever since that first morning in the skies over Greece, the thug had been bragging to everybody about his willingness to become a martyr. Now one moment of hesitation was followed by another, and before Abdul himself knew what had happened he was backing away from his own death. The human animal had taken over the program.

Jones almost felt relief as he was dragged to his feet and jostled over the lip of the berm and down a slope that was waist high with spring grass. It looked beautiful, the green blades waving in the slight breeze. *God, I don't want to die this morning. This is a shitty way to die.*

He wondered if the trooper who had flashed past on the motorcycle had been hit by any of the return fire. Jones hadn't counted the number of Kalashnikov caps that had been busted. The truth was he'd heard little over the swishing of the pulse in his ears.

As they rushed down the slope, Abdul wore him like a second skin, his beard scratching Jones's face, the man's breath hot and fetid.

"Do as I say," Abdul hyperventilated, "and you might live."

Jones was reassured by these words. The man's thoughts were focused on living, not dying.

"Halt!" someone cried in Arabic from the berm above—and then again in what Jones thought to be Farsi.

Fiercely, Abdul clutched on to him around the neck. Jones could scarcely breathe.

"Don't move," Abdul wheezed in Jones's right ear, then screamed at the American who had risen and was carefully treading down the slope: "Go back, or I kill this man!"

"Like you did his buddy in Algiers?"

"It was your rashness that killed the Marine Hale. Go away *now,* or I shoot this one too!"

"You do it," the American said calmly, "and I'll ship you to Allah with your pecker sewn in your mouth."

Jones could feel the angry jolt pass through Abdul's body. This was bad news to a devout Moslem, who planned on enjoying the maidens of paradise. The Marine knew the American was just buying time, hoping for a shot to open up. But he was powerless to help him—Abdul was clinging to him with vicious desperation.

"So go ahead and shoot," the American went on in the same imperturbable tone. "But before you do, I want you to know who will be preparing your body for the funeral—Major McCoy and Sergeant Major Peterson, United States Army. And by the way, Amal brigade headquarters fell about half an hour ago. That's how Peterson and I learned about your little junket to Bekaa, Colonel Abdul."

Jones realized by the way McCoy had twice emphasized the name Peterson that he was trying to alert the second Delta man to what was happening. But the Marine could see no one through the thickening pall of smoke. The motorcycle rider must have been picked off.

McCoy had begun to sidestep in search of an opening, but Abdul froze him in his tracks by screaming, "His brains! I will shoot his brains if you do that again!"

His heart hammering, Jones felt no doubt. The major was stymied. He could do nothing without getting the Marine killed. And Jones himself had no question but that if he even flinched, the lights would go out, concussively.

Suddenly, catching Abdul off guard, the second Delta man popped up out of the grass. Incredibly, though, he didn't open fire. He just stood there, his pistol in his hand hanging down at his side. It was almost like he was saying, *Go ahead and shoot me.*

Abdul turned to react, and Jones felt the man's body part from his a few inches. A single round was fired, and Abdul's shoulder jerked like it had been hit. Jones sensed that the shot had come from McCoy, but the terrorist's stunned attention was already directed on Peterson—so Abdul went ahead and fired twice in that direction.

Peterson went down into the grass. Jones elbowed Abdul hard in the gut. And, as McCoy loosed a two-shot burst, the Marine dived for the ground, burying his face in his hands, expecting to feel a sledgehammer blow in the back any second from Abdul's Beretta.

Silence.

Jones rolled onto his side. McCoy was standing over Abdul's body.

The major then glanced down at the Marine, who nodded that he was all right.

McCoy took his knife and cut Jones's bindings, then strode toward where Peterson had disappeared.

"All right, Peter, what kind of idiot trick was that? I saw two rounds bounce off your Kevlar. Welcome to the sore pectorals club . . ."

Jones was halfway to his feet when the major made a sound like he'd been bayoneted, then spun around, throwing the Marine some kind of miniature transceiver. "Medevac *now!*"

"Who do I talk to, sir?" He approached the two men and grimaced. Peterson had taken a bullet through the throat. His face was only a shade darker than the whites of his eyes—but he blinked once. McCoy was applying direct pressure to the wound.

Jones knelt beside them. "Sir—who do I raise!"

"Big Boss—tell him Little Boss wants a Sea Stallion now on the Damascus Road. Four or five klicks east of Aley village. Tell him the LZ will be marked by smoke.

Tell him to put Doctor Jack aboard!" McCoy was trying to stop the vivid red arterial flow with both hands now. "Do it for me, man!"

The radio operator on the other end promptly answered, and someone who called himself Alexander took the horn: "Who's hit?"

"Your man Peterson."

"Who are you?"

"Lance Corporal Jones, sir."

"Where's McCoy?"

"Busy with Peterson, sir."

"Okay, tell him I've got a chopper on the way."

Wiping his damp face on his sleeve, Jones glanced up at the road, where the other hostages had queued on the berm, their bound hands held before them as if they were praying.

Peterson began choking on his own blood. Gently, McCoy rolled him over to clear his air passage.

"Back over, Scotty," the sergeant major rasped after a moment. "Can't breathe this way."

"How's that?"

Peterson parted his lips to grin—his teeth were coated with frothy blood. "Arlington . . . a room with a view."

"Bullshit!" McCoy changed palms on the wounds, his hands now stained red all the way to the wrists. He looked up, trying to wipe away the tears on his shoulder. He screamed into the smoke-darkened sky, "Where's that chopper!" Then he turned on Jones. "Where's that fucking chopper, you son of a bitch?"

"I don't know, sir," Jones said quietly.

29

Doctor Jack grabbed Alexander by the arm. "Boss—you've got to help me."

"McCoy?"

The medic nodded. "I finally got him to stop arguing that Pete's still got a pulse. With a blown carotid? He was gone before I ever made it up there in the chopper." The man took a sharp breath to steady his voice. "Shit, Pete was my friend too. McCoy's not the only son of a bitch on this plane with a hurt in his fucking heart."

"Don't take what he says personally. Okay, Doc?"

"Yeah, yeah, but McCoy won't let go of his hand. And I've got to get Pete in a body bag before we land."

"Let me handle it. How's the hostage with the leg wound?"

"Okay. I got him zonked on morphine in the upper bunk. The frag did some damage to the soleus. More pain than anything else."

"Thanks. You've done a hell of a job, as always."

Laboriously, the colonel climbed the flight deck access steps.

One glimpse inside the small cabin convinced him of what he had refused to admit to himself for some time: McCoy was finished. This operation was going to be his last. It wasn't that the major had nothing left inside. The point was that, over twenty years, he had already given too much.

"Hello, Scott."

He was grasping Peterson's hand with both his, which were stained with dried blood.

Alexander avoided looking too closely at the body on the lower bunk. Otherwise he risked sliding into the same

195

condition McCoy was in. He honestly didn't see how the sergeant major could ever be replaced. Peterson had been like connective tissue binding the diverse personalities of the force together. And, more than that, he had been a hell of a human being.

McCoy had been crying, hard, but now he had stopped.

"It's time to let him go, Scott. Let Pete go."

"I can't."

"Yes, you can."

McCoy pressed the dead hand to his forehead. "No."

"Then tell me why you feel you can't."

McCoy's answer was completely irrational. It also made perfect sense. "If I let go, it's all gone for good. Papa Emile's . . . the early days at Bragg . . . Half my fucking life is gone."

"That's right. It's time for you to let go of those things."

McCoy shook his head obstinately.

Turning, frowning at the interruption, Alexander saw that one of the hostages, the one named Kaplan, had stepped quietly into the cabin.

"Yes, what is it?"

The old man's eyes moistened as soon as they came to rest on Peterson's body. "I know this is no time to bother you. But I must, you see." He lifted his chin at the lower bunk. "I must know his name."

"What the fuck does it matter to you?" McCoy asked, not looking up.

"I'm a survivor. I survived the Holocaust. And I can't stand the idea of a brave man dying without a name. So many died with no names."

Alexander nodded. "He was Sergeant Major Peter James Peterson."

"Thank you." Kaplan started to leave, but then he stopped and turned again. "Freedom from fear," he said very deliberately.

"Pardon, sir?"

"I said *freedom from fear*— that's from Roosevelt's Four Freedoms, remember?" The old man smiled sadly. "The hardest thing about surviving what I did is seeing how quickly everybody forgets. They worry about the mortgage, fancy cars, a vacation in Florida each winter. They're so utterly free from fear they don't even know what real fear is. Anybody who even mentions the subject is called an alarmist. And all this only makes me afraid again. I can't breathe. It's going to happen all over again, I tell myself. There won't be enough selfless men and women to stand up and say, 'No, we will not let things go this way. We will not turn the world over to madness and terror.'" He wiped his eyes with a handkerchief. "Well, I am not afraid this morning, gentlemen. *I am not afraid.* And the Benjamin Kaplan family mourns the loss of your friend. God bless him for his courage. Excuse me now . . ."

Alexander watched the old man withdraw, then looked to McCoy again.

At last the major had let go of Peterson's hand. After a long moment, he said, "Do me a favor, boss."

"Name it."

"Get Mr. Kaplan back in here. And Lance Corporal Jones too—I gave him a ration of shit he didn't deserve. I've got a favor I want to ask both of them."

30

29 June 1985 . . . 1400 Hours . . . Arlington National Cemetery

McCoy held Nancy around the waist. Once she had begun to slump, and it had taken all the strength in his left arm to keep her on her feet. After that, she seemed to do better. Her nine-year-old son held on to her dark skirt. He was not Peterson's child, of course, but no one could have told that from the devastated expression on the boy's face.

The sergeant major's mother and father were standing on McCoy's right side. He had picked them up this morning at the airport. Frail, both in their late seventies, they were not up to this. Their grief made them seem confused, distracted—as if they had no idea why the President of the United States was standing on the other side of a hole in the ground from them.

In his own mind McCoy now questioned whether it had been wise to summon them from their hometown in North Dakota, "a one-water-tower burg out nowhere," as Peter had described it.

Nevertheless, all of Peterson's loved ones were being spared the ordeal of national television coverage that Thomas Hale's family had endured in order to say good-bye to their son.

To protect the identity of its operators for future covert operations, Delta made sure that its funerals were private affairs, except for a highly select group of VIPs.

Looking down on the Lincoln Monument, his eyes bleared, McCoy thought, *Well, here's the view you asked for, brother. But, had it been my turn and not yours, I would've asked to be buried with my other face pointed toward Washington.* He chuckled softly to himself, then tried to cover it with a cough. Distinctly, just for an instant, he had heard Peterson's laugh. It hurt to hear it, even in reverberation.

Eyes right.

The casket was being borne toward the grave by six pallbearers—not the usual honor cortege for a military funeral.

Scott McCoy came to attention. He squeezed a hand in his each of his: Nancy's young one and Mrs. Peterson's old and bony one.

Carefully, he studied the pallbearers as they approached.

Waukene Winnemucca, his face stone, his heart probably lodged in his throat, although you'd never know it by looking at him.

Bobby Lee, tears streaming down his face. *It's okay, let them know we're just ordinary men when not called upon to do extraordinary things . . . Let it flow, Bobby, all the way down this green, velvety slope to the Potomac.*

Nick Alexander, looking tired as hell.

One of Peterson's wheat farmer cousins, uncomfortable in his suit coat and tie.

Lance Corporal Edward Jones, in Marine dress blues, expressionless, moving with perfect martial grace.

And then Benjamin Kaplan, looking saddened but proud—looking as if it all meant something.

It was while gazing at Kaplan that McCoy finally smiled, although he had to press his lips together to keep them from trembling. He could go home now to his forty acres of pine and pasture—and without the bitterness eating at him like acid. Peterson had been right about this one. It had all come together.

Now that you've enjoyed this book, discover other exciting paperbacks from St. Martin's Press